Never Take Advice From An Unscarred Man

Dennis P Kolb

Order this book online at www.trafford.com
or email orders@trafford.com

Most Trafford titles are also available at major online book retailers.

More of these adventures are true than I care to admit.

Printed in the United States of America.

ISBN: 978-1-4269-7629-2 (sc)
ISBN: 978-1-4269-7630-8 (e)

Trafford rev. 07/29/2011

 www.trafford.com

North America & international
toll-free: 1 888 232 4444 (USA & Canada)
phone: 250 383 6864 ♦ fax: 812 355 4082

THE STORIES OF DENNIS P. KOLB

The following story introductions are divided into three parts. More than one introduction may apply. Hopefully all three will apply.

STORY INTRODUCTION NO. 1
FOR THOSE WHO HAVE EXPERIENCED.

These stories are meant to be read slowly and again, thinking back over the miles and years. The stories are meant to revive old memories and put them into the perspective in which they belong. Memories are a warm walk looking at yourself through smiling eyes at the funny mistakes you made. Everyone made those mistakes, so everyone can enjoy the trip.

You can choose the easy road this time through. Remember to turn the sour to sweet as you travel along. The pains need not be endured this time. Look at those tough times as the winner of a race looks at his painstaking preparation. Baby it was worth it! Now let's see you do it, and congratulations if you do.

The stories are purposely condensed for pondering on your own. You were not alone.

STORY INTRODUCTION NO. 2
FOR THOSE EXPERIENCING RIGHT NOW

These stories are to be read as your struggles continue. Make note of them, ride them out, and laugh at them. Forget the bad parts or make them fun and cherish the challenges that memories are made of.

Each new challenge should be invited, just to see what will happen. Stubbed toes don't hurt so bad the next day. None of us has done everything there is to do. If failure comes, so what! It was your first try. It's a great excuse and experience. That failure has spotted some of the bugs that can be worked out. If it was too painful, there's a million other adventures out there. If nothing goes wrong, it's a dull day.

STORY INTROCUCTION NO. 3
FOR THOSE WHO WILL EXPERIENCE

Usually, you are the young ones. If you are afraid to be laughed at, you are going to miss out on the best of times. Strive to surprise yourself. It makes you a leader. Guts shows. Watch the old guys and stay away from some of their most painful mistakes. It's always nice to live to be older. Fear motivates kids to greatness just as fast as boredom. Think up your own game rather than play someone else's. It gives the old guys laughs now, and you'll get to laugh later on. Life gets better every day.

IT'S SUCKER FISHIN TIME

When some people mention deer hunting as their favorite time in Wisconsin, I scoff at their mistake. If they had ever been sucker fishin with me, they would throw rocks at hunting the whitetail in sub-freezing temperatures. Oh sure, it can get a little uncomfortable when you happen to fall in. But heck, that can happen during deer hunting too.

During the winter, I often stop to check that the rods are set up for the early sucker run. I wouldn't think of catching them any other way than hook and line.

Early in spring, as the Wisconsin winter loses its grip, my dreams are full of plump suckers being swung onto the bank, at Kolbeck's bridge.

The snow melts, filling the ditches, which in turn, fill the Little Eau Plaine River. We are there to watch the river rise, swelling over its banks in places, as the ice jams its progress. It can't be long now.

At home, we can see everything happen in line. All the snow melts off the garden, and the mud is just over boot deep. It's parsnip time.

The first day the mud cracks, there is a flurry of activity. It's about the first of April. We check Kolbeck's Bridge almost daily, waiting for the ice to go out.

We are finding the first worms. The sinkholes on the road to Kolbeck's are in full bloom. It's time.

When we were digging worms for this special season, we classified all our worms into four categories; too small, night crawlers, your regular angleworms, and our special 'pajamas'. Our special worms were sturdier than your regular worms, but much tastier, to the fish, than night crawlers. It took a trained eye to weed out the losers from the worm can. Armed and ready, we were on our way.

We had watched the tricks of the older fishermen over the years. We had tried each trick, and rejected the useless ones. Some of the dandies, included spitting on the worms, or putting them in your mouth to keep them warm. Another useless piece of advice was, 'Throw it our farther'.

The most interesting sucker fisherman I ever came across was Clarence 'Butch' Kremer. Butch would always catch fish. If he came to Kolbeck's while we were there, we'd watch his every move. He'd look at the water, walk along the bank, check the wind or something, and he'd know if it paid to throw in a line. If he left without fishing, we'd go home.

I've seen Butch sit there on the ground, and catch his big ones, one after the other, while no one else had any luck. Other fishermen would inch ever closer even tangling in Butch's lines, without getting a nibble.

Butch did have a snag problem, I saw him progressively solve. Every time his line broke, he'd put on heavier line. I remember, especially, the smile he had on his face, fishing with 100 pound test line. He sat there in the mud, the black smoke swirling through the open windows of his 53 Chevy, in the warmth of the tire fueled bonfire. Ah, here was a man who could enjoy himself.

Another time, back in the woods to the east, we ran across an old guy who made a big splash every time he cast, but never got snagged up. He had a six inch length of chain tied on for a sinker. I never went fishing without my chain, after that.

I hadn't gone sucker fishing for a couple of years, when two fellow workers asked me to go along with them. It was a good time. I would not have missed it for the world. Let me tell you about it.

It was near dark when we got to Bradley Bridge, just east of Stratford. Dave Munch, Karl Kohnhorst, and I were ready for some serious fishing.

While Karl and I were bent low over our poles, in the light of the gas lantern, watching for the slightest twitch, Dave was having a big picnic lunch. Dave was sitting on a pail close to the bank's edge. His poles were on rod holders down in front of him.

Karl and I had each caught a couple by now.

There was a big yell to our left. I looked up just in time to see Dave leaping backward, stumbling over his pail, and hear the riverbank, that had been in front of him, wash into the drink, rods and all.

Dave quickly grabbed a stick, belly-flopped on the ground, started poking around in the mud below, and lamenting over his lost rods. I could hold my mirth no longer, and cackled till my sides ached. He did not find either rod.

On the way back to the car, Dave, dejectedly carried his leftover lunch, the worm bucket and the lantern. As we neared the car, there was an ever increasing acrid burning smell in the air. Karl suggested, "Somebody must be smoking some rotten stuff." We all laughed.

Then Karl happened to turn around. He let out a yell.

"Hey Dave, you're burning a big hole in the worm bucket with the lantern!"

The Styrofoam bucket had an oozing hole melted in its side. My sides were aching again, as I doubled over with glee. Dave smiled a little, because it wasn't his worm bucket, but couldn't see the humor I did.

"Shut up, Kolb, my worm bucket is shot, and my lantern's got goo all over it!" Karl barked.

That was it, I couldn't stop laughing till I was exhausted. Never, or hardly ever, had I come out on this end of the stick. It was indeed, a memorable day.

It had finally come to this after all these years. It would be downhill from now on. I remember all the years of sucker fishing, when my equipment was the butt of so many jokes. I could catch fish all right, but something was always wrong with my rods. I would wash them in the river quite often, but they still malfunctioned. I'd cast out hard, and sometimes, only five feet of line found its way out of the reel. The six inch hunk of chain on the end made other fishermen give me a wider berth.

"The End"

THE OLD OUT HOUSE

All through my growing up years we had no bathroom, furnace or running water in the house. Don't feel too sorry for me. Had this not been the case, I might have gone through life with very little to write about.

As primitive as this may sound, we were not hampered in any way. In those days it seemed quite natural to go to the bathroom outside and cook inside. Nowadays it's quite fashionable to do it the other way around.

I remember the old toilet with genuine affection. I remember the first one as being a fine three holer. There was some philosophical writing on its venerable walls. "Some come here to sit and think, but I come here to _____." This bit of literature was passed to the next privy in line.

It could be a chilly seat in the winter. Our mother fastened felt across the whole works and it was quite comfy. The pail of wood ashes in the corner provided the janitorial service. A sprinkle of wood ashes on anything offensive, immediately leaves any odor mute. When regular toilet tissue was not affordable, as can happen with seven kids, a catalog served its dual purposes. There was also a stick in the corner, that some sadist always turned upside down, that we will not talk about.

In later years, when I learned a little about electricity, I even installed a battery powered light.

The little building faced toward the north just behind the house. With the door open, there was a fine view of the northern sky at night. Of course, if the door was open, it meant that, since the door swung to the inside, you could not get the door shut without getting up.

Don't get ahead of me.

Every morning, long before us kids were required to stir, my dad was performing his ritual with the door propped open, to welcome the new day. Great things were planned during these morning meetings of the mind.

This one morning things were a little different. Though it was 6 A.M. someone drove in and turned to park by the house. Not 25 feet straight ahead was a frantic man trying to get up, gather his overhauls from around his ankles, and get the door shut in one smooth motion. His personal observation later was; "What did them damn fools want at six o'clock in the morning, anyway?"

We used to tell stories of things we'd seen living down there in the hole. It used to make my sisters nervous as the devil. Personally, I didn't believe any of it.

My mother's Uncle Ed used to come to visit around the first of July every year. I guess he was a pretty good old guy, but kids just naturally exploit any weakness in character that they detect. Kids made old Uncle Ed nervous. We proved to him that he had every right to think the way he did. Once, he was in the old biff and we locked and braced the door. It just so happened that green apple season was in full swing. The orchard was right behind the outhouse, and served as a handy target area using the toilet with Uncle Ed tapped in side as the target.

Uncle Ed had a problem with his voice. When we let him out, he went straight to my mother to tell of his imprisonment and subsequent bombing attack. He was much too excited to make it clear what had happed to him. We apologized to him before he had a chance to rat on us.

All through grade school it was something of a status symbol to be one of a few who didn't have a bathroom in the house. As I got into high school, I became embarrassed of the situation, as any kid in that age group is likely to do. I didn't want the other kids to know that I wasn't rich. Heck, you might even call us poor because of that blasted outhouse. I never invited anyone, but when one of them found out about it, he though it was great. So, how do you figure?

One day I was sitting in the old john just contemplating life in general. Something touched my behind! Holy Smoke! I was on the dead run just inside the outhouse door. Somehow I was on the move, streaking to the north with my pants around my ankles. All those stories of snakes, spiders, rats, and strange animals of every sort whistled through my mind in that instant of being touched. My imagination, being what it is, enhanced an already frightening situation. After about twenty yards, it became apparent I was not being perused by my attacker, so I quit yelling and stopped to pull up my pants.

I warily snuck up on the house of fear. I kicked the door, and it whipped open with a satisfying squeal of the hinges. I grabbed a shovel and bolted through the door. Nothing. Then I looked down the center hole and there it was. The damn cat. The filthy thing had licked my butt! He got me in the end.

By Dennis P. Kolb

"GESUNDHEIT!" OR "YOUR HEALTH!"

Over the years I've noticed how sneezing has filled an otherwise void part of my life. It can be used as and excuse, weapon, repellent, and can be highly entertaining as well.

There are all kinds of sneezers out there. Some are gentile, some barbaric, some muffled, and some spontaneous. Others are quite colorful when physical accompaniment is added.

The timing of a sneeze usually seems like an act of God, or perhaps His supreme adversary, old Lucifer himself.

It is said, we are closest to death when we sneeze. From my own experiences, I can voucher that, at the very least, pain is close by.

A faked sneeze can be used to suggest an oncoming cold. Kids don't use this much because their mothers figure the rest of the kids in school deserve a pay-back for all the sicknesses passed on to their own.

Adults, however, overuse the sneeze as an excuse. They use it to get out of unwanted situations. They use it to get through a big crowd; much like the faked imminent upchuck. It's used to demand more breathing space or moving space. Faked sneezes are hardly ever used for entertainment and I think that is a shame.

Honest-to-goodness sneezes can spray fear, embarrassment, and glee into the hearts of the observers. Be watchful. Don't miss out on the fun. Your eyes will be rewarded. You'll see someone like me, frantically looking for a place to set down a brimming cup of scalding coffee as the mother of all sneezes wells up like a flash. There is a 50-50 chance that I'll go un-scalded. This is always an early morning adventure so it's a good gage for the rest of the day. It has never happened more than once a day. Thank God!

I'd really enjoy being the audience just once, instead of the victim over and over and over. My wife has long since stopped enjoying the scene. The laughee shouldn't have to clean up the mess if he's providing the entertainment. The entertained didn't see it that way. She has another proverb for this situation: "He who is idiot enough to sneeze with a cup of coffee in his hand, best clean up the mess!"

Looking back, there was one incident that will stick in my mind as long as I shall live.

It was a Sunday morning, in church at Saint Michael's in Hewitt, Wisconsin. My brother, Vernie, and I were next to one another in the pew. I was in the final stages of a winter cold. You know, when all the crap is cleared out when you blow your nose. It's kind of a disgusting time. Nine and ten-year-olds lack finesse in these formative years. They also lack laugh control in the House of God. Everything funny is heightened to a fevered pitch whenever church is involved. At the end of this Sunday morning, the insides of our mouths were raw from trying to put a clamp on our mirth from the inside.

It all started quite innocently. I sneezed. Of course no handkerchief, or even a cupped hand, was there to catch the discharge. The discharge landed on the coat of the lady in front of us, about half way down. The revolting chunk hung there boldly.

"Holy smoke!"

I had to do something. Maybe I could pick it off there, when she sat down.

Vernie was shaking in silent glee. I elbowed him. He only got worse.

The slight chance came as she sat down. I reached for the vile hunk. Too slow! Half my arm was caught between her back and the pew. Her startled recoil was enough to let me pull free. I'd come up empty-handed. I dared not look at Vernie. He was retrieving something from under the pew, I think.

My ears burned because I knew that somewhere a nun's eyes had to be boring into the back of my head. I rubbed away the pinch from my arm and thought some more.

The next time the slimed lady stood up, the offending glob was gone. I mean we couldn't see a trace of it anywhere. It had blown the scene. It was history.

Where did it go? Who knows. This is not the sort of path traveled by miracles. But it was gone.

I can't think of a graceful way to get out of this story. I'll just go blow my nose.

"THE END"

PICKIN THINGS

When the snow was gone it was time to start limbering up the fingers for the picking season. The winter break is over. Everything that was frozen down is thawed and ready to be picked.

Sticks and stones are the first things to be picked in the spring. The lawn and garden are cleared of these things as soon as they are loose. The work delay of a late spring is dear to many a kid's heart.

The next thing to be picked raises the spirits of many a kid, young or old. Angleworms look pretty good about the middle of April. Sometimes, half the garden is spaded by the time we're sick of fishing suckers and bullheads.

Wild flowers take their turn in the picking cycle as spring takes over in Wisconsin. We are foolishly, looking forward to picking more things. The wild strawberries are blossoming.

We knew where every wild strawberry grew within a three quarter mile. We knew where the biggest ones grew, and picked all the patches in cycles. It took a long time to fill up a cottage cheese carton with wild strawberries. It got a little disheartening, to see half a days work disappear in less than five minutes at the supper table. Over the years, many hours were spent picking, and blowing the road dirt off of, pints and pints of wild strawberries. The gritty berries added body to the mix and nobody seemed to mind.

The garden started to show signs of things to be picked. By the end of June, the dreaded bean picking started. Into the third and fourth picking, whole bean plants have been known to disappear entirely. By the seventh picking, depending on the picker, whole rows might be gone. As good as buttered green beans are, the chance that I may have to pick them, forces me to break off a plant or two, as I walk through the garden. It actually made me look forward to picking wild raspberries.

Wild raspberries grow in places not always comfortable to normal human beings. My mother and my aunts were avid berry pickers. The conditions we picked under were mere trifles to them. The bugs, briars, heat, and wild animals seemed to be overlooked altogether.

There were some incidents through the years of raspberry picking that made it tolerable. My aunt Alice could pick extra fast and tell great stories at the same time. I remember her talking half an hour, to a bear, she thought was her sister, before the bear walked away.

My aunt Mabel could pick a six quart pail full faster than I could pick two and a half quarts on a good day. I think maybe her daughters helped her fill her pail just to show me up. I always tried to steer clear of such show-offs.

Standard picking gear consisted of a long-sleeved shirt, a straw hat, bug dope, and one of my dad's old ties to hang a lard pail around your waist. Warm pop or lemonade and sandwiches were doled out when the kids who were along on the day's operation, started dropping from hunger. They were always amazed to find some of the lunch already gone.

I remember going on a picking excursion in my aunt Helen's new Studebaker. Four kids and two adults made up the picking party. There were Mitsie and Mary Lois, their mother, Helen, our mother, and Vernie and I. Picking parties always filled the car.

When we had enough picking for the day, all the kids headed for the car. We had not been in the car long before a big dog was jumping at the new car, barking his head off. We tried to duck low so he would go away, but he kept right at it.

It was a long time before my aunt and my mother showed up all out of breath. They had found some berries, they couldn't pass up, in a pasture next to the woods we were picking in. It seems they were not all that occupied the pasture. A large bull had tested their stamina and speed. They had managed to roll under the fence and escape.

Back at the car, they chased away the dog, and surveyed the damage to the paint job of the new car. Uncle George would be fit to be tied when he saw the side of his new maroon football.

Ever optimistic from their escape, they wet down and dusted the scratches away. They actually got away with it.

Blueberry picking wasn't too bad until I stepped on a bee's nest. I got stung so many times so fast that even my eyes swelled shut. Mud does work to get the swelling down, but it doesn't take away the bee phobia that has been instilled in the flick of an eye.

Blackberry picking is where you really get to know your surroundings. A blackberry briar can grab hold of you and keep tearing at your body, till it draws enough blood to excite the mosquitoes into a frenzy. The best berries always require their pound of flesh.

Picking corn was a pleasant change. Getting a chunk this big in one piece made me wish berries grew on cobs, then we wouldn't have to pick the little suckers, one at a time.

It has been a long time since a berry pail hung down in front of me, but not quite long enough to make me miss the sensation.

Apple picking was always done one at a time, just before eating it. The only exception to this rule was in the throwing season. This season lasted from the time the green ones were big enough to sting their victims, until we got tired of it, or hit something forbidden.

The forbidden hits might include anything from a neighbor kid or a window, to a passing motorist. A stray apple could lead to a warm butt, in a hurry, back in those days.

Pretty soon everything froze down again, and the picking season was history for another year. Thank God for the changing seasons.

"The End"

HOME MADE TOYS

A kid without cash can lead a normal life with the help of a creative imagination. Once this resource starts working, the options are endless. It is very important, however, to make sure the direction taken is not toward destruction.

The first idea of the day is a good indication of how dangerous it will be. Ideas expand quickly. Only bodily injury stops the chain of steadily increasing threat. Beware of animal ideas in the early morn.

Most homemade toys are already there. We didn't have Frisbees, but we had plenty of tin can covers to sail. Tin can shoes were all the rage out our way. Aluminum would never stand up to the abuse tin cans took. These were good early morning toys.

If you started off a rainy day leaping off the beams in the barn, into a small pile of straw, suffering was certain. This was okay late in the day, but never in the morning.

An unlikely toy was the electric fence. To make this the most fun, a gullible kid was required. We experimented with the fence, so we knew what was dangerous and what was merely risky. A piece of grass was risky and a wet wire was dangerous.

A windstorm took down some telephone wires, providing us with some great experimental equipment. If we strung a piece of telephone drop wire from the electric fence to the coaster wagon, we had a dandy trap for a gullible kid. The rubber tires on the wagon provided the key. If you hopped into the wagon, the fencer's jolt was avoided. If you grabbed on to the side of the wagon, however, while climbing aboard, the sting from the fence would gurgle up your arm. It took almost a week to run out of gullible kids, with the wagon trap.

Once in a while, a kid is found who seemed to be on the brink of lunacy. Even then, the trick would only work one time. Making water on a charged fence creates high notes only certain animals can hear. A kid gets to see this only once or twice in a lifetime, so it's very special, indeed. I'm not mentioning any names, here, on purpose.

One day, a bonanza was bestowed on us that provided entertainment for weeks. We were given a bundle of unprinted yard sticks. It's incredible how many things a yard stick can be used for. Even today, I use them in imaginative cobbling. We made the usual swords and daggers, of course, but there were many other toys hidden in those sticks. There were car ramps, kite parts, bike wheel noise makers, planes, things to shove in exhaust pipes, body slappers, to name a few. Sometime, when no one is looking, grab a yard stick, and hold it like a tin can cover. Now, throw it like you would the cover. If you do it right, you'll get a satisfying whirring noise out of it. Go ahead, try it again.

Kites provided their share of thrills. We made our own. About the only decent string we could find was on my dad's cane fishing poles. Our kites dived a lot unless the tail was so long it would barely become airborne. As time went by, we got a couple of bough ten kites. These weighed less than the binder twine we used to hold our homemade ones together. We borrowed my older brothers casting rod to give us the height and convenience it required to hit the big time.

You could hardly see the kite, it was up there so high. Then it seemed to be moving. The fishing rod was dancing along the ground and picking up speed as we raced after it. Then it came off the ground, just higher than our flailing arms. If it hadn't been for the elm tree on the line fence, it might be going yet.

The nearby railroad tracks were a kid's paradise. The rocks were perfect for throwing and the signs were great targets. With a yardstick for a balancing pole, you could walk a rail till you tired of it, or till you heard a train whistle. I was quite young when the last of the steam engines went through on the tracks, past our place.

The diesels were not as loud, and could surprise you. I remember putting things on the rails to see what the train would do to them. Coins were flattened beyond recognition. Small rocks were pulverized.

Only once did I feel in any danger, playing on the tracks. A couple of my brothers were playing where the track crossed the road. I joined in the fun. My foot slipped into the space, along the rail, and I couldn't pull it out. I could, however, slide it along to the end and get it out that way. A diesel horn wailed. He was bearing down on us. I still had six feet to go sliding my foot along the crevice toward the approaching train. My brothers were trying to help me with furious body english while the engineer was camped on his horn. Those little hairs on my neck stood out like nails, as I slid my foot toward eternity. I'm not sure if it was as close as it seemed, but it was somewhat less than ten seconds, left to spare. My brothers thought it was a funny time for a kid to puke.

Playing Annie Annie Over in the fall sharpened up our throwing skills for the snowball season, that was not far off. If you could hit a moving target with a rubber ball, or a rotten vegetable, you could hold your own on the field of battle.

Snowballs are as homemade as you can get. It took about three days of good snowball weather, for the nuns of St. Joseph's school, to forbid any further war games, in Hewitt, for the duration of the winter. There were still small skirmishes on the playground, and an occasional snowball bomb that came out of nowhere and dropped real close to a vigilante School Sister of Notre Dame. Everyone got punished for a simple act of God, like that.

We still had some decent wars at home, so our skills were not lost.

We didn't have computer games and snowmobiles, in those days, but no one missed out on action and fun. We had home made toys.

"The End."

MAKING DEALS

Making good deals was the only way a broke kid could keep up with his more affluent counterparts. Sometimes it was necessary to take advantage of any sensed weaknesses another kid would display. Curiosity was the downfall of many a rich kid. Most of us held our own in the bargaining arena, but I have a brother who developed it into an art he still hones today.

If Paul wants something you have, you are dead meat. You would be better to give it to him outright, because by the time he is finished with you, he'll have what he wants and you'll owe him a favor, to boot.

I've seen Paul toy with people just to sharpen his skills. He was not above offering a man, with a stalled car, less than a ten dollar bill, to take it off his hands.

I guess I started noticing his talent quite early in life. With a dollar for seed, he could grow a new, or slightly damaged, bike or sled. Paul used another kid's pain like a lever. While everyone else asked a kid if he was hurt, Paul would reach in his pocket and offer him a paltry sum for the toy that hurt him. This kid was borderline genius in making timely deals. I sometimes questioned the ridiculous deals he tried to make. Paul claimed he didn't have to be successful one out of ten times to come out ahead.

Paul must have a file system somewhere just to keep track of all his ongoing deals. If you needed something, and were willing to wait, both he and you could benefit from his skills. Of course, this meant you owed him one.

Patience was Paul's strongest suit. Patience needs to be nurtured to become a powerful tool. Give Paul a four by four, and he'll carve you a link chain out of it. He and I even carved an Indian head out of six foot stump, using chainsaws and chisels. Paul hand carved a nine foot muskellunge, just to crank up his bargaining skills.

You won't get a fight from Paul if you are the type who keeps offering to pick up the tab. This is an idea I have used a number of times, myself.

Before I start giving examples, I have a couple more of the areas of bargaining to explore.

When going to look at an advertised bargain, there are several steps to consider. Don't ever take a new vehicle if you don't want to pay top dollar. For God's sake, look as dumb as you possibly can. This is easier for some than others. Wear a hat. I'm not sure why, but Paul always wears a hat when he's bargaining. Maybe it's to hide his shifty eyes, never the less it works. Pretend you are doing the guy a favor, taking the item off his hands. Don't keep all your money in one pocket.

This last area of bargaining is by far, the most important. This is the one used car salesmen use with such skill. The person you have just shafted has to go away with a smile on his face and a song in his heart.

If you screw someone, and they are not pleased about it, you may never get a chance to do it again. If there is raucous laughter erupting in the area where there is bargaining, another sucker is born.

I'm going to try to show the extent of Paul's bargaining skills, exhibited a couple years ago, on our yearly smelt run to the north.

Our younger brother, Pete, had backed out on the morning we were to take off. Of course that meant a share of expenses were gone too. Paul had worked all night and had a dumb, tired look about him.

I should have expected something right away. He knew I waited for this trip all winter.

"Maybe we should just forget it for today." Paul taunted. "I've worked all night and with Pete not going, it'll cost too much."

Wow, he had me right where he wanted me. Is this guy good, or what?

"I'll pay for all the gas if you drive!" I heard myself say.

He transformed into an energetic gear loader right before my eyes. To this day, I'm still glad I paid for all the gas. Talk about bargaining skill, and I know I got suckered in.

We stopped at a grocery store for munchies, and I swear he got a better deal than me.

Before we had gone thirty miles, it was snowing. The weather didn't stop us from bargaining wherever we could along the way.

We stopped at Annie's Bar in Marengo, about thirty miles south of Ashland. Annie always calls when the smelt run starts, and we always stop to give her some business and a friendly hard time. She was in good bantering form.

Paul went out to the van and brought in his hand carved, and painted, two foot crappie. It is a beautiful piece of work. For leaving it on display, at the bar, Paul bargained us a few free drinks. It felt good to get some of the benefits of his skill.

I was so pleased to get those free drinks, that I bought our supper when we got to Ashland. Wow, he did it again.

Paul said he could use some sleep so we pulled into a wayside area next to where the fishing would be done, in the next few hours. For a solid two hours Paul slept. The snoring was impressive. It

21

looked as though he might even loosen the headliner, as he sucked in air, form time to time. Finally the deafening noise and vibration woke him up. The truck would not start. He had left the lights on.

Paul forgot he was wearing his joke hat, that revealed he knew Jack someone, before he stopped a passing motorist to ask for a jump start. I was sitting in the van watching the lady passenger check out his cap. I was laughing too hard to catch her full reaction, and was still doubled over when Paul climbed back inside. The mirth was contagious when he realized the reason.

He put on a bargaining hat and got someone to give us a jump. We gassed up and went to church. Looking at the nasty weather was all it took to decide to buy whatever smelt we wanted and hit the road home.

We stopped at Annie's to lie about the good fishing, get a couple free drinks, pick up the crappie, and be on our way.

We were home at a decent hour, and successful too.

"The End"

THE PONY JUDGE

Nothing can hurt one's image quite as quickly as being asked to judge who is best among friends. It is a no win situation any way you look at it. So it was, when I was appointed to judge Bratt Mitten's three oldest daughters in a dry run Pony Show.

For many years I had blamed Bratt for setting me up for such a kill. I t was a surprise, when I found out who the sadist was. I had always thought Bonnie as being such a sweet innocent little girl. You never know.

This would be a test of character no sixteen year old kid should have to endure. At least two, and maybe all three, little girls would be unhappy before the show was over. If I judged with my heart instead of my head, they would not be fooled. They would know that little Mary couldn't take all the honors, it was her first show. What if Chris was best all the categories, she was the oldest? If she won it all, Bonnie and Mary might be scarred for life. Our little show was only a week away. I would have to think of something.

Chris's confidence was overwhelming. I would have to try to even the odds somehow. I would have to do it honestly. It wouldn't be nice to spook Chris's pony, for instance, just to make her lose. Heck, she had feelings too.

I've got it! I would help Bonnie and Mary get their ponies ready, myself. We worked the ponies every day as Bonnie and Mary improved their skills. Mary no longer looked like a beginner, as she put Dolly through her paces. The little gray filly was learning quickly. By the end of the week, the participants of the show all had a shot at winning.

I worked up a list of points to judge each phase of the competition. There were points for grooming, the stand and stretch, the pony itself, trotting, backing, horsemanship, style, poise, and one for honorable mention. Since going through this judging ordeal, I can no longer tolerate an incompetent judge.

On show day all the ponies were scrubbed and their manes braided, and trimmed with ribbons. They looked great! If the judging consisted of appearance alone, we had three winners.

The first part of the show was the stand and stretch. I was glad to see Mary's pony edge out Tiny and Lacey. Dolly was stretched out like a pose in a magazine. This could be close.

The second part of the show was the individual competition. Chris put her pony through her paces. It was nearly flawless, but I was a tough judge. Bonnie and Mary Kay had their work cut out for them. Bonnie was next. She showed even better horsemanship, though Lacey wasn't as deft as Tiny. I was impressed. Now it was Mary's turn. She did very well. If Dolly would have had a few more lessons it would have been even closer.

I was closely scrutinized as I added up the points. There was no way to get out of publishing the results.

Chris won Best of Show. It didn't seem to surprise her at all. She was always confident, but never unfair. She expects success, but will work as hard as necessary to achieve it.

Bonnie won the Horsemanship award. Bonnie worked hard, but was always a little surprised by her success. She could have won it all with Chris's pony, possibly. A little fearful of rodents perhaps, but generally a dependable young lady, who's fun to tease.

Mary won Honorable Mention. If her sisters were not competing against her, she would have won at the pony show to come. Mary is the most sensitive of the three, but would fight to the death in something she believed in. She has a hidden fire that could bring her to fame.

When the ponies were entered in competition the results were the same, except that they beat everyone else. I knew I was a good judge. I would not do it again.

Growing up with these kids, and their four younger sisters, has been a puzzling experience. It's been like having seven best friends. They know they could ask for anything but nobody takes advantage on one side or the other. You have to be careful what you ask for, because someone may not say no, when they should. Just don't ask me to judge nothing.

"The End"

MAIL ORDER MEMORIES

Catalogs display dreams like Kim Bassinger displays bathing suits. The colored layouts and lovely models have a way of creating a want in the most mundane shopper. There are no malfunctions, weaknesses, pain, or missing parts in these displays. Some of the glowing attributes in the written descriptions picture these items as no less than magisterial.

I must admit to being sucked in more than a couple times. I'd hesitate to admit this, but I'm not alone in the gullible department. I've been to garage sales where these miraculous devices abound. If it's not sold in stores, it usually winds up at a garage sale.

One of the bigger items I've seen purchased from a catalog was Bob Gibbons' motor scooter. I remember helping rip the crate apart in my parent's garage. The crate contained the scooter, all right, but it was not ready to ride. There were bags of parts and instructions in four languages, English being a mere afterthought.

In less than a week, we had the beautiful baby blue bubble-fendered brute ready for fueling. Hardly any parts were left over. We were proud of ourselves.

The motor scooter would make us independent. No more groveling for one of our parents' cars. No more having to disconnect the speedometer, so we wouldn't rack up miles. No more trying to explain how we burned up a three quarter tank of gas in fifteen miles. These would be great times, indeed.

We mixed the gas and oil to fuel the new scooter. Each tank-full was good for about 50 miles, according to the broken-English instructions. Don't believe everything you read. I can just see some sadistic moron conjuring up these lies.

Since it was Bob's motor scooter, he would make the test run, solo. The engine started almost at once. Bob was ready. The maiden run was underway. Ten feet into its first voyage, the scooter's bubble fender was viciously attacked by the gravel driveway. In turn, it wrestled Bob to the ground in payment for the nasty scratches in the new paint.

We were not deterred for long. We threw some dirt on the fender to cover the scratches, and we were off, amid the scornful cackling of my younger brothers and sister. No bantering bozos could detract from the pleasure we felt as we tooled down the road with the wind in our hair and a song in our heart.

Soon it was my turn to drive. We took the blue beauty along the railroad right-of-way since we didn't have it licensed yet. The scooter was in rare form as we whizzed through the tall grass. Coming from the right-of-way, back on to the road, required speed, to make the grade. I cranked the throttle. The front wheel didn't touch the road again till we got into the ditch on the other side. With our wipe-outs out of the way, we were ready for the road.

With no license on the scooter, we had to be careful and a little deceitful. This was tough for me, of course, but Bob had no trouble with it at all. We'd wait till dark, push the motor scooter out of parent's earshot and motor away to distant places. Dodging cops proved easy, remembering the 50 mile range of the gas tank was a little harder. The reserve tank never took us near enough to a gas station, and the thing wouldn't run on lime vodka. Since fuel was so costly, and our wages as pinsetters at the bowling alley so meager, we did not find enough cash to ever license the scooter.

Most of my mail order purchases these days, consist of electronic gadgets. The price is usually low enough to make them disposable. Sometimes, I am pleasantly surprised. Other times, I have acquired a garage sale item. There is always an unlimited supply to choose from.

Books are a big mail order item, and can be costly. Book-of-the-month clubs can saddle you with a dead horse that in no way has a contents portrayed on the cover, or in the description. These mistakes don't bring much on garage sales. Buy it where you can browse it. Classic books are pretty and impressive. But some of these authors' works do not impress everyone who reads them. I might say, I could get more out of the book report they sell in the book store. This means you keep the book because you paid so much for it, but it doesn't get read.

Kids have the corner on mail order music. My son has enough in stock to play continuously for at least ten times as long as anyone would care to listen. If it's loud, he's got it.

I've never had the guts to try mail-order clothes. It's hard enough to buy things that fit from the rack. Besides, everything seems to shrink after a few months, lately. The hit-and-miss would further tax an already tough life. Of course, you can send it back. Shoes by mail must be a real adventure. I can go in three different places, and depending on the brand name, require three different sizes.

Beware of catalogs that offer sweepstake chances to patrons of their wares. They sell the kind of stuff you throw in, to try and sweeten deals of garage sales, without actually adding any value. Auctioneers sell this junk by the bushel for fifty cents a crack.

Mail-order insurance and credit cards are an amazing commodity. They rank right up there with the instant loans through the mail. These make a strong case to get rid of bulk rate postage altogether.

I enjoy catalogs of all types, whether I buy from them or not. If I could continue getting the catalogs without buying anything, I would get every one I could find. But alas, after a few catalogs with a last chance warning, they quit coming.

Probably the roughest lesson I had in mail-order concerned a complete bolt-on dual-exhaust system for my old pickup. I read about the advantages of dual-exhaust with increasing interest. I could use more power, better mileage, and smoother operation. These were all but guaranteed by dual-exhaust. I decided I could afford the mail-order variety.

A fellow worker said he would wait to see how I fared. If I was successful, then he too would install the same system. I would be his guinea pig.

The exhaust kit arrived. Bright and early, on my day off, I started working on the exhaust system. It was quite pleasant, working under the truck, on the soft grass of the front lawn. In half an hour I had the old system completely removed. I was half done.

Just before dark and nine hours of agony later, I had the new system installed. Nothing fit like it was supposed to. My knuckles were raw. My vocabulary was exhausted. Parts were missing. I had to make three runs to town to buy tools and parts. I was not a satisfied mail-order customer.

Back at work, I was quizzed as to how the installation had gone.

"Piece of cake. I did it right on the front lawn."

His system took two mechanics, four hours, with a hoist and a cutting torch, to install.

"That's funny. Maybe you got a bad one."

"The End"

BUTCHERING MADE FUN

This is not a story for vegetarians in general, though you may decide to become one. I heard someone say, "If you wanna eat meat, something's gotta die." That quote pretty well sums it up. If this is the case, somebody has to do the killing.

I got to help snuff chickens as soon as I displayed a steady hand and a strong stomach. The first time I was chased by a big rooster, provided plenty of killing instinct. Roosters' get mean if they get to be a year old. Oh, I'm sure there are pet roosters out there who are the picture of docility. Personally, I've never seen one. I was well acquainted with attack roosters, however. Hens and old clucks can get nasty if you try to snatch their eggs, but they don't go looking for trouble like old roosters.

Some chicken catchers use speed and bare hands to capture their prey. I preferred to use tools, and in extreme cases, firearms. A chicken hook I used was an ordinary clothes hanger molded into a catching machine. First, take all the bends out. Now, bend the business end into an 'R', with the left side of the 'R' extending to the handle. The chicken's leg is supposed to end up in the eye of the 'R'. Personally, I wouldn't use anything but a landing net, but as a kid this was a luxury.

Once the chicken is caught, you have a handful of feathered fury to subdue. Once the wings are clamped to the legs, you have momentary control. You are ready for the kill.

Now, the chopping block and hatchet come into play. The chopping block should be big enough to need splitting if you were to burn it, and flat on both ends. The hatchet should be sharp enough to make a relatively clean kill. Any more than two swipes with the axe are considered in poor form.

Now, the chopper grabs the rooster's comb and stretches the neck over the block. Whop! It's over, unless the holder lets go of the freshly beheaded chicken, either accidentally or on purpose. Now, the fun starts. If there are no obstacles to speak of, the chicken can really get going. My mother frowned on this. She claimed it bruised the meat. I always figured it was worth it.

Meanwhile, back at the house, water was boiling over the stove. A couple dips in the scalding water, and the feathers came off pretty easy. The smell of a wet chicken is memorable.

For a little more excitement, the chopping and holding can be done by the same person. Two spikes hold the head in place for the execution.

I always left the gutting to someone else, so this is the end of the lesson on chickens.

Rabbits and squirrels butchering was a simple method. Saw through the hide, rip it off, jab a hole in the belly and scrape out the guts.

The minor job of getting all the hair off and the rest of the innards out, was left to the cook. I had the dirty work done, he was dead.

The firearm proved to be a vast improvement over the hatchet, even on chickens.

I bought a hundred pullets one time to get in on the big money in eggs. There is always a rooster or so in a batch of chicks. We had one. He was safe and happy until he tried to stop Shirley from gathering the eggs. Now he was in trouble. After the third attack, Shirley refused to gather the eggs. The rooster must go. His reign was over.

I grabbed a coat hanger and headed for the coop. He evaded me for a long time, all the while putting the hens in a frenzy. When he flew straight at me, I flailed him off. That was the limit of my patience and compassion. The feeling had accelerated to hate and disdain by the time I returned, to the coop, with the gun.

I stepped into the coop. The stage was set, not unlike the old west. The hundred hens were on the sidelines, the rooster boldly standing in the center. The fool had come to a gun fight without a gun.

I could have gotten by with the 22, I thought, as I slipped the shell into the 12 gauge. At fifteen feet, this will be the fastest butcher job on record.

I touched off the Ithaca. The chicken coop exploded. The noise was deafening. There were chickens everywhere. Where's the rooster? Holy smoke! It took close to ten minutes for the feathers to quit flying. I still couldn't hear. Oh my gosh, what about the hens? Will they ever lay eggs again? Will I ever hear again?

The dust cleared, and I could make out the shape of Herman's crumpled carcass lying against the wall. I figure, after that, the rooster deserved a name. Anyway, I picked the sucker up by the leg and tossed him onto the roof, as I stepped out the door. Herman was history.

My hearing came back in less than an hour.

Just after breakfast, the next morning, I mustered the courage to see what effect the blast had on the hens. To my pleasant surprise, there were more eggs than chickens. Near as I can figure, the hens knew Herman was a non-producer, and didn't want the same medicine. After that whenever production fell, I'd walk through the chicken coop with the gun.

Shirley claimed I was loony, but I swear the old girls picked up the pace.

The bigger the animal, the more fun goes out of the actual butchering. That's when the spectator in me takes over. Why, I could watch it half the day, I think.

We still butcher a few chickens every year, but the fun is kind of stifled. Shirley is afraid I'll let the chicken go, so she won't let me be the holder. What's the matter with a few bruises, heck, other entertainment costs more than that.

I guess the main lesson I learned over the years is the size of gun to use inside a chicken coop. A twelve gauge, or any shotgun for that matter, should not be detonated inside a small, closed building.

"The End"

WHITETAIL BY GUN

I had hunted the wily whitetail by bow for a few satisfying years, not successful, just satisfying. This would be my first gun hunt. No longer would they be out of range. I would bloody my virgin knife, no sweat.

Roger Gennett suggested I join his party in the hunt. A brother-in-law wouldn't steer you wrong. He said it would be a great time. Why not? What kind of equipment does it take? Where do I get a license? Good questions all, and pretty expensive questions at that.

Woolworth's had everything I needed, as I shopped, the night before the hunt. The Winchester Model 94 30-30 looked good, so I bought one of them. The red clothes were over budget, so I settled for a red hat and a red vest. A box of shells and a license later, I was equipped. My sister knitted me a nice brown cap with a white tassel, but the regulations said I had to wear red during the hunt.

This was about the time I realized gun hunters were a breed apart. We had to get up in the middle of the night, drink coffee, talk smart, and be on the road by 4:30 in the morning. I was only good at half of these requirements, and never this early in the morning.

Some of the roads we were driving on as we neared Pray, made the name of the place seem appropriate, indeed. Cars were parked on both sides of the road, some in the ditch, with barely a car width in between.

I was dressed like a mummy, as we started our long trek into the woods, in the dark. By the time we had walked the eighteen or so miles, back in the woods, I knew these gun hunters were downright strange.

Sweating like a pig, in the 20 degree weather, I slumped against a stump and ate all my lunch. These guys are nuts!

About thirty seconds before first light, everybody within two miles must have emptied his rifle. It was like a war zone for the first half-hour. I tried to dig a foxhole with my bare hands to no avail. Making it through the whole day without being shot was a real plus.

On the way back to the car, the distance had dwindled to less than a mile. Tomorrow had to be better. Before we got to the car, I shot at a tree just to make sure the gun would fire.

We were back at the war zone early the next day. So far, I hadn't seen a live deer. Back at my stump, I settled in for a little nap. All these guys say they never sleep while hunting, but I've noticed some strong signs of grazing, where these fellows were sitting.

I woke up about 9:30, yawned and stretched, and noticed a little buck watching me. I picked up the gun and shot him. Every body converged on the scene. I explained how I had stalked the monster for an hour and a half, and shot from the hip while he was running full bore. Roger told me to cut the crap. He said he heard me snoring way over where he was.

We got it gutted and hung on a tree. Right about this time, I started to realize why Roger wanted me along. The other fellows in the party either developed a physical impairment, or disappeared altogether, as it neared time to go home. Roger and I dragged the deer the eighteen or so miles to the car. Everyone appeared just as we hoisted the kill onto the fender. Roger lived in Spencer, so I could tell any story I wanted, around Marshfield.

Early Thanksgiving morning, our new hunting area was the McMillan Marsh on the Spencer end. We made arrangements as to where everyone would be, so nobody could be in the line of fire. I got turned around anyway.

I was relaxing on my stand when there was a rustle to my right. The biggest deer I have ever seen stepped into the open. I raised my rifle. He needed to go to my left to be out of the line of fire to another in our party. Instead, the big racked devil, headed trotting towards the other hunter's stand. After he was a long way off I stepped out into the open, only to find out I had my directions screwed up. I didn't feel so bad when Roger's dad, Mark, came over by me sporting a wet leg. "I just saw the biggest deer of my life!" He said. "I couldn't get to my gun!"

It's funny how that old deer could tell that I was lost and Mark had his zipper down.

Roger shot one before we left and he and I dragged it out. I suggested he just flip it up over his shoulders and I would carry his gun. He gave me a dirty look. "Why aren't you wearing that stocking hat Mary made for you?" These gun hunters are a strange lot.

"The End"

POETIC JUSTICE

Have you ever seen someone get their just deserve? I have. It's one of the highlights of my life. It's great! Let me tell you about it.

Having served my four plus years in Uncle Sam's Navy, I had seen more than my share of unreasonable, snotty, people. It always seemed, when a person felt power, he felt the need to abuse it in about the same proportion to his undeserving of that power. It was sad to see them get away with treating people like dirt. These clowns needed reprisal.

On this night, all my frustrations from these years would melt away in one fell swoop. It says in the book of Genesis that God made the rainbow to lift the spirits after a storm. My rainbow was on its way. I would see an obnoxious fool foiled.

One evening, not long after I met my wife, we were sitting in the Patio Restaurant over pie and coffee. We were enjoying ourselves when a portly, hell, fat guy came in with a big chip on his shoulder. He looked the place over, and finally took a booth for himself.

Tubby was grumbling steady from the time he sat down. Nothing suited him and he hadn't even ordered yet.

"Clean up this mess." He ordered.

The waitress was doing her best to appease him.

He ordered his food. The waitress was barely out of sight before he started in again.

"Are you going to take all night?" He growled. "Where's my coffee? At least give me my coffee. Do you think you can handle that?" He snarled, so everyone could hear.

The waitress was almost in tears. She was hurrying around, gathering all his special requirements. She brought his coffee, cream, water, and silverware.

"It's about time." He griped. "You'd think you had a hundred people to wait on. Don't expect a tip for this kind of service."

I was really disgusted to see and hear this kind of abuse on someone who didn't deserve it. I wished someone would treat him the same way, just one time.

The waitress had run to the kitchen to compose herself before his next onslaught. We could see she hated the day she had come to work here. Bozos like this don't happen in every day, but once is too often.

Bozo stared at his coffee. Then he put some cream in his coffee.

"Hey, this cream is sour." He ranted. "Bring me a new cup of coffee and some decent cream."

The waitress hurried to comply with tears in her eyes. He just glared at her when she set down the new coffee and cream.

Bozo stared at his coffee again. He poured in the cream without grumbling. He didn't see the sugar.

"Where is the damn sugar?" He snapped. "What kind of a joint is this?"

The sugar containers held about three cups of sugar, poured through a hole in the heavy screw-on lid. The waitress pointed it out; right in front of him.

He grabbed the container and turned it over above his coffee. I didn't see all that happened next because my hair trigger went off about half-way through and I couldn't stop laughing.

The loose heavy lid and three cups of sugar displaced the coffee in Bozo's cup instantly.

"Eeeeiiippe!!!" He yelled, as his lap was washed in hot coffee.

I could not see what happened next. I was having one of those uncontrollable laughing fits, where the tears blot the vision. Shirley dragged me out of the booth and ten feet away to where the jukebox stood. In a minute I thought I was under control.

Not yet. I looked back to see him swatting coffee off his pants. I grabbed hold of the jukebox and shook uncontrollably with glee. When Shirley saw it was no use, she grabbed me and ushered me out the door. While I gaffawed till my head ached in the parking lot, she ran back and paid our bill. We got in the car and I kind of settled down. We must have gone seven or eight blocks before we stopped at a light. I looked at Shirley. "I didn't think it was that funny." She said. I started all over again. The car behind had to horn me back to reality.

We tried to sit and talk in the driveway before Shirley was to go in the house. It was no use. I only made her angry with my bodacious outbursts. Finally she just got out and went into the house.

By the time I got home to bed I was finally laughed out. My head, stomach, and sides ached but all the frustrations from a long time past were vented, thanks to Bozo.

Every time I see a customer give a worker heat, I wish for some of Bozo's justice and a smile of anticipation waits.

"The End"

I GOTTA HAVE A JOB

After working for Uncle Sam's Navy, and a stint of welcomed unemployment, I moved into the work force. My work record, was a little shaky, working for a couple electrical contractors, a cheese company, and a job wiring mobile homes.

Currently, I was working for the General Telephone Company. Working with phone installers was kindred to electrical and familiar, so I was not sent directly to the line crew to work in the muddy trenches. A new recruit, getting this kind of break, angered the cocky line superintendent, Ron Hawky, but he would have his day.

The inevitable time came and I was to learn the ways of the line crew. The work was dirty, the hours long, but Hawky made the most of his chance to make it miserable.

In between, I got a breather, for a week, selling extension phones that were installed free, and cost a dollar a month, thereafter. Hawky followed up and sold where I didn't to get me off the gravy job, and back under his thumb.

It was twenty below 0, and we were working in Colby, just east of the Colby tavern, looking for a broken cable in a ditch that was, somehow, filled with water. We were poking around with our shovels, looking for the cable.

"Kolb, get your butt down in that ditch." At –20, and nowhere to go once I was soaked to the waist, I suggested we get a pump and get the water out first. It was 20 miles to Marshfield.

Hawky was hot. "Get your ass down in there, now!"

The other fellows watched, as I thought about it for a minute, tossed the shovel onto the bank, said "---- it!", and started walking down the road. Hawky was right after me. "What did you say? What did you say?"

"I said ---- it!", and I kept on walking back to Marshfield, except for a ride part way, with a compassionate motorist.

After I left, as later told, he called Elton, gave his story, and then went back, got a pump, and pumped out the water to find the cable.

When I got back to the shop, Elton, Hawky's boss, was waiting for me.

"Why did you walk off the job?" I told him. He pressed for a better reason.

"It was either walk off the job, or hit the s.o.b. with the shovel. Which would you rather I did?"

"You better look for another job, Friday is your last day." was all he said.

Fellow workers rallied on my side to no avail, so I was down the road without a job, and set to be married on Saturday, the 25th of January. I would have to move fast.

I had previously applied at the Marshfield Electric and Water Department so I headed there Wednesday, right after work. I had been to Navy Electrical School, served over four years, and I could do the job.

I walked in the office, told Lolly my application was there, and asked if there were any openings right now.

"I'm sorry, no." She said.

"Well, I've got to have a job. I get married on Saturday, and I just got fired!" I pleaded.

This statement brought Norm Dietrich right out of his office.

"Come in here once," he said. "Bring along his application, Lolly."

I told the whole sordid story, while Norm and Lolly listened.

"Yes, that's the way that man is." Said Lolly, my head snapping in her direction. Mr. Dietrich looked at my application for a long time. Finally he looked up with a smile and a twinkle in his eye.

"It looks like you are qualified for everything, including the top job at the power plant. All I'd have right now would be a job on the coal pile, and you'd have to work up from there. Interested?"

"Yes Sir!"

"You will need to talk with Kenny Graff, get a physical, and be ready to come to work as soon as these things are taken care of." He said.

I would later find out Lolly had worked previously for General Telephone, and Bratt Mitten, one of my character references, was a good friend of Norm.

I lined up and passed, a physical with Dr. Doege at the clinic.

Early the next week, after the wedding, the utility office called for me to come to work. My mother told them I was working for the phone company, but gave them my new phone number.

No one, besides Shirley, knew I did not have a job on our wedding day. I finally got the message, and started shoveling coal at the MEW on the fourth of February 1969.

I never realized how much story material this new job would provide.

"The End"

JUST MAKE AN EFFORT

I bought the old green pickup for $90.00 from Mid-State Truck. When the salesman said I could buy any parts I needed, at a discount, I should have known what to expect. But I still had a truck and on the night shift to boot.

I was actually able to drive it home, which was a big plus. I needed a pickup to haul things and go places. These two requirements were a tall order for this vehicle.

To make the truck a little safer, we got the brakes working on all four wheels. While it was jacked up, I wrapped a tin can around the exhaust pipe, making that part of the system like new.

The heater fan, radio, wipers, and emergency brake hadn't worked in a long time. I replaced the broken windshield with a used one for a measly forty bucks. I got over half of the lights to work at one time. I was proud of myself. Maybe this wasn't such a bad buy, after all.

I found a rear view mirror so I didn't have to crank my head around so often. It would have been nice to have an outside mirror too, but luxuries would have to wait.

Norm Simm helped me put in a new carburetor kit. The engine was hitting on at least six or seven cylinders now. If it hadn't backfired so hard, the tailpipe might never have blown off. If I was real careful the noise wasn't too bad.

The tires had no tread to speak of, but maybe I could find some used ones before winter. I never worried about a blowout, cause I was afraid to drive it over 40 anyway. I was still searching for one component that was in perfect working condition. I couldn't be sure about the alternator. It could have been the battery that was bad.

During those learning years, the authorities were real hot on safety checks.

I was driving the old green binder into town when I was nailed dead to rights in a state safety check. It was merciless. I could have gone to lunch while he was writing up the violations. He even ran out of ink, and had to run back to his car for a new pen. I was slumped over the fender waiting for the bad news. I checked the sky, to make sure I'd get home before dark. Finally he was done.

He handed me the list of violations. I read the bad news while he stood and watched me wince every once in a while.

"Do you think I should just park it, and walk away." I said.

"No," he said. "You've got five days, just make an effort, and I'll be satisfied." My guess is, he didn't want the junker cluttering up the street.

Where to start first? I fixed all the lights except the dash and interior lights. I fixed the horn. I bought a new windshield wiper motor. I put on a complete exhaust system.

On the day of the inspection the binder wouldn't start. I went to see the inspector, and he gave me another five day reprieve.

I was really whittling the list of offences down. A little more work, and I could trust to take it, maybe ten, fifteen, miles away. Things are looking up.

Since the mechanical problems were coming along so well, I thought I'd have a crack at the dents in the body. I worked for two days, carefully getting most of the dents out. Now, for the rust spots.

I was using every specialty tool I could find. I had a mall, a pick, hammer, pliers, and a couple screw drivers to boot.

I got a big pile of sandpaper and went to work on the rust spots. Things were really going well. The good door was the part I would finish first. It had no dents and just a couple of small rust spots.

"Hmm, looks like a little hole here." I mumbled to myself. I brushed the spot with the sandpaper, and a hole appeared as big as a cat's head.

I snapped.

My hand brushed the mall. I grabbed it and started swinging with loud verbal accompaniment. It took almost half an hour to beat the tailgate off before I could get at anything else. It was as though all the frustrations, from a long time past, were being vented on this beastly truck. I put every dent back in, that I had removed, plus a few more. I leaped up on the roof, and put the new windshield out of its misery. By the time I was done jumping up and down on it, the hood was resting firmly on the engine. Back on the ground, I grabbed the pick, and stuck it in the door.

The instant rage ended as fast as it started. The truck was junk, but I would never have to work on it again. It was the most satisfaction I had felt since I had bought it. I gave it to my brother to junk or use any way he liked.

It was nice to tell the inspection officer, the fate of the green binder.

No one can say that I didn't make an effort.

"The End"

WHAT ARE SCOTTISH HIGHLANDERS?

The new frost of the quiet fall morning gave no hint of what the new day would bring. Today would be a day long talked about for many years. Lessons would be learned by some of the people involved that would never be forgotten. These stories vary a little, but I shall try to set down a version that will, more or less, tell what happened that day.

Bratt Mitten acquired five purebred Scotch Highland cattle. These cattle have long reddish-brown hair and horns a couple feet long. They're bred to thrive in the highlands of Scotland. These babies are of sturdy stock. Bratt enjoyed having things that were not too commonplace.

Bratt had been working up to this for years. There were fantail pigeons, Bantam chickens, goats on the roof, a runaway roasting hog, and geese on the road. He even acquired a variety of wild animals and took the show on the road. He had champion ponies, ducks, and dogs without manners. It was not dull.

Bratt's main business was the greenhouse. He worked long hours and tried the complete florist trade. Having mastered all phases the hard way he fulfilled his philosophy. "If it's not worth learning the hard way it's not worth learning, cause you won't remember it." Bratt remembers lots of stuff, let me tell you. By doing a lot of two man jobs alone, he majored in creative vocabulary expansion. Ah, he was a master teacher, and I was usually, just a step off his heels. By the time my navy career started, I could teach sailors new and inventive phrases to astound their friends.

Bratt let the cattle out into the corral before I got there, that morning. Soon the action started. A few fences were destroyed and the roundup had begun. The long hair on those beefers faces kept them from seeing fences real plain. Each new fence they destroyed, only irritated them a little more. Where they came from, the fences were thick cables.

The situation was gradually getting out of hand and accelerating. Cattle were running everywhere. People were reporting buffalo on the road, while we were chasing some of the hairy devils cross country. Action breeds bravery, and I soon had one by the horns and wrestled to the ground. Soon she was haltered and tied to the bumper of my almost new truck. The tail light was swiftly smashed with a swinging horn. We drove out of George Eberhardy's field with the heifer in tow. It was so easy. Piece of cake. It won't be long now.

The stage was set for a new scene. Bratt was working on one about a mile away as the crow flies. He had it cornered. She reeled and charged in close quarters. He grabbed the horns and pulled her down, the horn stuck in the ground. He sat on her head until help came with a rope. Another piece of cake.

Here comes this confident dude with his trusty halter, fresh from success, and brave to a fault. A few spectators had gathered by now, none of whom showed a lot of bravery of their own. An insurance man, a part-time game warden and a couple of others watched from a safe distance. Mr. Varsho and I walked to a small field where another heifer was breathing hard from her long run. Armed with the halter, I stepped into the open where she could see her target real good, even through all the hair covering her eyes. "Come bossy, come!" I teased. Here that suckers comes!! Nowhere to run!!! Too late!!!! "Arrrghh!!!!"

The horn caught the fabric at the crotch and ripped it cleanly to the knee. She never broke the skin or her stride as I went up and over her back. Everybody cleared out within a hard run away.

About this time, Bratt had his heifer hogtied and taken care of. All the excitement in the little field made him decide to call the County Mounties with some heavy firepower.

In half an hour we were ready. The officer took steady aim at a spot between where the eyes should be. Less than twenty yards. Piece of cake. No sweat. This won't take long.

"Bang!" Puff of dust! "Wow, bounced right off!" Somebody yelled. She wiggled her head and stared at him. "Brrrr!" The cop had kind of a funny look as he ejected the shell. His head jerked a little when somebody yelled. "Wait till she turns her head!" For a man holding such a large rifle, he did not look so cocky now. The second shot, to the temple, was true and quick. All was well.

About this time, Joe Koshnick, Bratt's old carnival buddy, happened on the scene. He was just in time to help load the animal into his handy pickup truck. All the wrestling and pulling, to get the carcass on the truck made him wish he had come a little later.

Soon a relieved, and partially victorious crew, arrived back at the barn. We had three live ones, one dead one and one gone. I wanted to be there but it was hard to be cool with my pants ripped at such a place. The other heifer would be caught later when she mingled with a farmers herd.

With the butchering done, Bratt took the huge set of horns to the taxidermist. It was not long before the taxidermist called. He had bad news. A dog had run off with one of the horns. Bratt didn't say too much to the guy on the phone. He put down the phone receiver and spent the next ten minutes or so in a very heated display of profanity. Wow, some new stuff, I'd never heard before.

He does have a nice powder horn he likes to have you ask about. Years have passed since those animals roamed on the Mitten farm but they will not be forgotten. I expect he'll have some great stories for the grandchildren. They say things heal and get funnier as the time tempers the wounds. It took a few years to laugh about these. The last I heard he wants nothing that eats or excretes. When all those past frustrations become funny, you won't be able to wipe the smile off Bratt's face.

Here is where I must confess of a lack of sanity. Remember those three live Scotch Highland cattle in the barn? Well, … "How much do you want for those three in the barn?" Bratt never flinched. "Should be worth two hundred a piece." "I'll take em!"

But that's another story.

By Dennis P. Kolb

WHAT HAVE I DONE NOW?

This story should not have a chance to start. Something must have snapped, or at the very least, stretched real tight. How did I get myself into this one? As near as I recall, it went something like this.

"How much do you want for those three in the barn?" Bratt never flinched. "Should be worth two hundred a piece." "I'll take em!"

My brother Vernie and I now owned three Scotch Highland cattle, two heifers and one bull. I would take care of them in Bratt's barn during the winter and build a corral in the spring.

One of these animals had just tossed me quite handily and had to be shot. Another was gone. I was part owner of animals who could not be trusted real far. This was real dumb. This could turn sour. This could be dangerous. Oh my!

Every day, though the winter the animals were fed and watered. Every third day their pen had to be cleaned. This was fun to watch.

There was a box stall in the corner of the barn. I had to get those big long-hairs in there so I could clean their pen. I'd show them some nice fresh hay, then put it just where they could see it back in the box stall. Then, a little feed was sprinkled on the hay. They were getting excited and pushing on the gate. Now, to quickly open the gate and stand back. They rush into the box stall. I'd close the stall door as soon as the last one was in there. When the pen is clean and bedded they are lured back. This got old by spring and the cattle earned my trust.

The corral plans were made and the materials were rounded up. I had to bust through frost to get the posts in. The posts were spaced eight feet apart and buried four feet in the ground. Three two by sixes made up the fence rails. The corral was finished by the fifteenth of April. We were ready.

We loaded the animals into Bratt's trailer backed tight to the barn. It was unbelievable! They walked along the aisle, and into the trailer. "Boy they've calmed down nice over the winter." What a relief!

We drove away to their new home. We backed up to the new corral happy with our good fortune.

Now, we need a little background here. This was the Kolb home place. Vernie owned a St. Bernard. This dog was full grown and he was impressive. Pabst was chained to his house with a long strong chain. We lived about an eighth of a mile from the railroad. After a while, you never even notice the trains.

We opened the door of the trailer. All three Scotch Highlands were quickly in the corral. Piece of cake. "I wish they would quit pacing." "Woof woof woof." The damn dog was straining at the end of his chain and thoroughly worked up. "Boowaa", the train warned the crossing. "Woof!" Too much stress!!

Two minutes to the second, two by sixes were flying. "There they go!" "Oh my God, now what?" Shirley said. "Well, do something!" Gee whiz, Holy Smoke, and Gosh Darn were all sayings that came to mind, but I'm sure you'll agree this called for more serious stuff, as the long hairs took off.

51

They ran about a quarter mile to the north, took out a few fences, crossed the road, circled to the west and finally were lying down. They were just two hundred feet from the corral, but just across the road and just on the other side of a fence. So close, but lets face the facts.

I called my uncle Mitch. "Bring your gun, I don't have one here." He came quickly. The animals still rested, but he didn't bring his gun. "Let's shoot them right there!" I said. He seemed surprised. Heck, we hadn't tried to round them up at all yet.

About this time, another train went through. Up, up and away they went. The five wire fence never so much as slowed them down.

The run was on. Maybe twenty fences later, two and a half miles away, they rested again along U.S. highway 10, just south of Hewitt.

The sharpshooters gathered, and were told where to shoot, to kill the beasts quickly. Traffic was moving and paying little attention. Two animals were quickly down, the other up and running. "She's going for the highway!" "Watch out for the cars!" Two cars just missed her and she was long gone. It was simple to see why cars hit deer. Some drivers have no idea what is going on near the roadway.

When I took Bratt's trailer back he wasn't surprised at what happened, but he thoroughly enjoyed hearing about it. I didn't think it was nearly that funny. He even made me stop in between. Said he couldn't take it, hardly.

Two weeks went by while we filled some freezers with meat.

Finally somebody spotted a buffalo. That's our heifer. Soon four by fours and rifles were on the chase. Shots were blazing, letting us know her progress. It was exciting. She was spotted across the miles. Dave Ott waited at a farm. "Here she comes!" He fired. Again, and again the rifle barked. On the fourth shot, and just fifteen feet in front of him, she went down.

The butcher was amazed. She took seven bullets before she went down. We had the whole thing made into sausage. I had over a hundred sticks of sausage hanging in the basement when all was said and done.

We did not receive one bill for fences destroyed. I will always remember that. It's good to know, if you provide fine entertainment, it is well appreciated.

So ends the second and last story of the Scotch Highland adventures. If you remember it a little differently, you could be entirely correct. It was a time of stress that tends to cloud things when they happen so fast.

"The End"

MIRACLE ON STADT ROAD

As I'm standing at our front window, Wisconsin is winding up another season. My mind drifts back over the years.

Soon after our son, Steve, was born, the doctors detected a hole in his heart. The doctors were surprised, when Shirley and I seemed to accept the news without emotional theatrics. They were sure we did not understand what they were talking about. Heart murmurs are serious business. They didn't seem to realize, he was our son, and we would be there no matter what.

The heart healed and Steve was a strong little boy.

My brother, Vernie, hobby farmed the home place. Steve loved to ride on the tractor with me, and was right there whenever the engine started. I guess the dangers seemed remote as he sat on my lap on the tractor.

Steve was riding along while I was disking the corn stubble in the field to the south of the old farmhouse where I grew up. We were having a good time riding round and round the field, getting ready to plow.

The Allis Chalmers WD has a foot clutch and a hand clutch making it seem to be as safe as can be.

It has been almost twenty years, but this story is still difficult to tell.

We were rounding the field, Steve helping me steer, as we headed toward the road, getting ready to turn before the ditch. Steve was hanging tight on to the wheel. We were going toward the ditch. I couldn't get at either clutch. I turned the wheel. He was still hanging on. I couldn't get to the brake or ignition switch. He swung to the left off my lap. I tried to catch him. I could not. He was sliding down as we turned. We were almost stopped. He's on the ground. Oh noooo!! We are stopped. He is under the disk. I remember my anguished cry as I leaped off the still running tractor.

"I've got to get it off of him!" "NOW!"

I reached down with one hand, grabbed the disk, lifted it high, and pulled Steve out with the other hand in one motion. I gathered him up and ran in shocked urgency toward the house, where Shirley and my mother were standing in disbelief.

My mother was too upset to think.

Steve was crying as Shirley gathered him in her arms and I raced to the nearest vehicle. Shirley seemed calm, but for me, the gravel was flying, and I was looking through drowned eyes, as I raced towards the west toward the hospital. Oh, why?

We were half way there.

"Let's go home." Shirley said. "But he was under the disk!" I wailed. "Just drive home." She was calm.

I drove home to 907 South Pine while she checked every square inch of our son. Steve was sobbing softly, as we pulled into the driveway.

Off came Steve's clothes to check everything. He had two pink marks on his chest. Not cut or red, just pink, where the disk had rested. He had a tiny cut inside his mouth by his lower lip.

I was in worse shape than anyone. To be so close to despair, then hopefulness, and finally complete victory, in such a short time, left a mark I shall never forget.

We called my mother and she could not believe that Steve had come through the ordeal unscathed.

I have always known that this was my personal miracle and no one could sway my conviction.

I tried to lift that disk later. It would not budge at all. Two men would have trouble lifting it.

Steve has grown into a fine young man nearing 21. The field where this happened has been our front lawn for over 17 years, so it has quite a history.

We hobby farm, raising animals and crops, besides working full-time jobs. Steve has never shown a big interest in farming and machinery, and we have not pushed it. He'll do great, with his attitude toward life.

You can never realize how much kids can be worth till you have their life in your hands. It's strange to know you would give your life at a moments notice to save their's. I can't wait till he has kids of his own so he can know that the best part of life is still ahead.

We have gone though a lot of tough times during the years since. Not much can get you down with a past victory like we've had. I'm beginning to see how obstacles in life make one strong. I can talk smart, I was granted one miracle, but it has taught lessons I hope I never forget.

Don't give up till you're dead. Nothing is hopeless. Life is precious, live it happily, and don't judge others harshly. God don't judge nobody till they're dead.

Steve thinks we sent him to college to get rid of him. He soon will realize how much preparation it takes, these days, to take on the world. He will then change his mind.

Dennis P. Kolb

OUR CAMPING DEBUT

Camping does not come naturally. It does not matter how many times you slept out in the backyard, or how often you went on a picnic to the park. It might have been a wise move for us to have camped out in the driveway, before we hit the road on vacation.

The main preparation for the trip was to get the little car ready to pull a camper twice its size. My cousin Gene fashioned a dandy trailer hitch out of old super heater tubes I salvaged from the scrap pile, behind the power plant. The preparation was done.

We would be leaving the comfort of our home to drive 500 miles, with a six month old baby, spending nights at camping grounds. What could go wrong? The little car was new and all of us were healthy.

I picked up the camper the day before we were to leave on vacation. The fender mirrors were adjusted to the limit so we could see past both sides of the camper behind. The empty camper was quite a load for the little Austin America. It took much longer than normal for the automatic transmission to reach fourth gear.

We started loading all the gear we'd need for a week on the road. We had to rearrange the gear when the rear of the car started to sag. By the time all was packed, we were gaining confidence galore. We were ready to go anywhere there was a road.

I kept my reservations to myself as we pulled away. The load on the Austin made it seem light on the front end. Thirty miles to the gallon would only be a memory, with a load like this. I hoped the transmission would take the strain of load and the 65 mph speed limit.

The little car proved up to the task as we headed south. The temperature gauge rode a little higher than normal, but still in good shape.

We had not gone much over a hundred miles before I made my first wrong turn. It's easy to get crossed up when you're trying to see the sights along the way. I finally stopped at a wayside when I was lost enough. While I pored over the map, Shirley explored the wayside and got a drink of water from the handy pump. Once I figured out where we were, we altered our route and destination.

After a little discussion on why we were lost, I got to do all the map reading for the rest of the trip.

It was late afternoon when we drove in the driveway of our first campground. The water from the pump at the wayside was taking its toll on Shirley's digestive system. Feeding the baby proved a lot less convenient on the road. Supper proved a lot less convenient on the road. Sleeping in a tent camper with a baby on a cool night proved very inconvenient. Diarrhea is not convenient anywhere, much less so, on the road. The only thing that kept us from going home the next morning, was Shirley's determination to forge ahead. I'd have bailed out.

Today we would see what Iowa had to offer. We picked a bad time. Everyone was cleaning their hog pens today. On a warm day, this activity lets everyone know what it would be like to live in a toilet. Wow, it made our eyes water!

We turned north and headed into Minnesota. The long hills proved a real challenge to the Austin America. We would be nearing eighty miles an hour as we neared the bottom on the hill, only to have the transmission shift down, as we neared the top of the next hill.

It was about this time we realized we were a wire short on the trailer light harness. We had no brake lights on the trailer.

We stopped at a store, bought some wire and a light, and proceeded to the nearest campground. I installed the new brake light, we had supper, and turned in for the night. We were serenaded by some people, whose talent for singing was found in bottles. The party died about one in the morning.

About two o'clock the storm rolled in. Wind and rain, accompanied by spectacular lightning, is much more impressive inside a tent camper. It was not a restful night. Each day found us less impressed with "roughing it". A comfortable bathroom took on a whole new place on our list of necessities, a couple spots above what had once been number one.

We hit the road again and headed north. We stopped in Gilbert, Minnesota to visit an old Navy buddy. After we left Oaki's house, we turned tail for Wisconsin.

In Duluth, there is a big hill as you approach the bridge to take you into Superior, Wisconsin on highway 53. On the way down the hill to the bridge the temperature gauge dove to cold, as I used the engine to slow us down. We were getting about 21 miles per gallon so far.

We stopped at Copper Falls. Wisconsin never looked so good as it did this day.

Back on the road, it was time to decide where we would spend the night. We looked at each other, and immediately knew the answer. I mashed the accelerator, and four hours later we were home.

Never again, would we envy the campers of America. I have many excuses ready just in case it is ever suggested again. How anyone in his right mind, would put himself voluntarily, in a situation like that, is beyond my imagination.

I would feel as though I was "roughing it" in a new motor home with a full bath and air conditioning. Anything less would be a hardship.

I can think of a lot of things I'd rather do than go traveling like we did.

❖ I'd rather clean out a calf pen.
❖ I'd rather smash my thumb with a hammer.
❖ I'd rather listen to an insurance seminar.
❖ I'd rather change a dirty diaper, and this one carries a lot of weight.
❖ I'd rather go back to grade school.

So there.

"The End"

GRILLED TO PERFECTION

My experience with grills began with the charcoal fired variety. My lack of experience contributed to the humbling ordeal. Long had I heard of the culinary masterpieces performed on these contraptions. It didn't seem necessary to take note on how it was done. How tough could it be?

Food took on a new dimension of taste and fragrant excellence when my brother-in-law, Roger, displayed his skill at the grill. He made it look easy. It looked like anyone could do it. It looked like I could do it. I was wrong.

My first grill was a simple table-model. Charcoal was added and my chef's career began. I washed the briquettes down with starter fluid. The match was still a foot away when everything was engulfed in flame. My wife just happened out the door in time to catch the wind.

"Are you smoking, again?" she asked.

"Maybe a little", I fumed. "You should have seen me when I was burning!"

My eyebrows grew back in less than a month. Since the lashes were only half-burned, they were like new in two weeks. The quantity of fluid to be used to start a pile of charcoal, was burned into my memory.

As soon as the flames died down, I put the chicken on to cook. After a reasonable amount of time, I moved the chicken from grill to plate. We felt like cannibals, trying to eat the raw meat.

Briquettes take a long time to get into the cooking stage. About an hour after our pork-n-bean feast , the charcoal was at its best. I turned the hose on the grill and steamed the life out of it. The grill hung on the garage wall from that day forward.

Years went by, and people were still proclaiming the attributes of cooking out. I must admit, when someone else did the cooking the food was great. It still looked easy. I've had some tasty morsels, from steak to brats, but I couldn't tempt myself for another go at it until gas grills appeared.

I was bombarded with the attributes of these cooking machines. They were foolproof. They started with the push of a button. They cooked perfect every time. An amateur would have no trouble at all. They don't use hardly any gas. They make everything taste a lot better. They cook really fast. Even an idiot can be a master chef.

I ran right out and bought a new gas grill, against my better judgment. After using it the first time, I ran down the list of attributes. I had to admit, the grill did not use much gas. My wife did very well, cooking on the gas grill. But there is an unwritten law that says, the man is supposed to cook on the grill. We sold the grill before we starved or were poisoned by my cooking.

I remember well, from my childhood, how we cooked in the house and went to the bathroom outside. How things change!

If a doctor told me I had to eat all grilled food that I cooked myself, I'd drop my excess weight quicker than I could say, "Toss me that can of grilled pork-n-beans and that crisp wiener". A pair of chore gloves, and I'd be all set.

I'm always flattered when someone is grilling and asks me to watch the grill while he runs to get a beer. It shows that not everyone thinks I'm a total failure with the grill. During this short trip to the refrigerator, I've seen a grill turn a nice piece of tenderloin into a flaming cinder. I've seen a potato explode with a vengeance. If I hadn't been asked to watch, these spectacles may have gone on unnoticed. What luck! You don't see that every day.

The aroma given off by cooking with grills could make a statue's mouth water. It would be nice if they sold air freshener ala grill scent. If the wind was right, I could fool the neighbors into thinking that I was cooking out. It has always bothered me that everyone would think less of me because of my culinary flaw. My brother-in-law offered that no one could think any less of me. Encouragement like that is really comforting.

It has always amazed me how grill cooking can be so successful. With the cover down, it's hard to tell when the food is on fire. Most of these cooks don't even have a garden hose handy. That's okay if a pail of sand is nearby, but you still have to wash most of the grit off the meat to get people to eat it.

Permanent markers make convincing lines on fried steaks but the less polite aren't slow to tell you they were not fooled.

I have found a way to get the best grilled food there is. Let someone else do it. Compliment them, beg them, and in extreme cases, pay them to do the cooking. This is a case where it is a great idea to throw money at the problem. If you feel that you are being overcharged, offer to watch his cooking steak while he runs to get himself a beer.

"The End."

THE LEFT STUFF

I learned very early in life that I was among a persecuted minority. Being a lefthander, I have endured the sadistic inventions designed to humiliate me. These inventions have been a sore spot for a long time and it's time I've had my say.

The next time you pick up a scissors, put it in the other hand and proceed. Isn't it strange the way it tries to gnaw things off? These instruments of insanity are made for north-paws. Unless the leftie learns to do it the strange way, he won't be doing it at all.

All through my growing up years, I have been plagued by contraptions that don't work like they should.

Even the saintly Sisters of Notre Dame had it in for me in the years I spent under their tutelage. Southpaws were frowned on and the Sisters tried to eradicate the defect as quickly as possible. She would put the pencil in the other hand and point the paper toward the left corner of the desk on every pass. Eventually, I quit moving the paper. I would listen for footsteps and become a right-hander when I heard them. Even now, I could use the wrong one, if I had to. My handwriting has none of the backhand look, thanks to the way the paper pointed as I outfoxed the nuns of St. Joseph's School, in Hewitt, Wisconsin.

When I got my first rifle, I noticed a very unhandy quality about it. It was downright clumsy. To load and reload a bolt action, single shot 22 from the wrong side is bad enough, try shooting an automatic without burning yourself. The empty shells, whizzing by cause a definite flinch. High powered automatic rifles or automatic shotguns might even bruise and burn at the same time. My old model 94 lever action ejected out the top but still deflected the shells toward me, ever so slightly. Hot gunpowder is always vented toward the southpaw.

Until a few years ago, fishing reels favored right-handers. Bait caster's still are weird that way but after my first one, over thirty years ago, I stuck with anything else.

Phones, car repairs, and bathrooms all have the north-paw in mind. In order to write something while on the phone it is necessary to change things around and fumble for a handy position. Car repairs are tougher because the engineers are right-handed and design the installation and removal of parts to foil the lefty. The next time you are in a bathroom check out where the tissue is. I rest my case.

Camcorders are the newest craze everyone seems to need. Many of these have eyepieces off to one side. You get one guess to figure out which side.

Cowboys have a heart. A horse is always mounted from the left side. If you try to mount from the other side, some horses will quickly correct your inconsiderate flaw. I thoroughly enjoy seeing this kind of punishment delivered. Being on the receiving end has made me a little cynical, at times.

I noticed they were real careful to make brooms and mops that even I could use. It's comforting to know there is a wide open field out there, if I have no talent for writing.

Pencils and pens are okay, but theme notebooks are made by righties.

Almost everything with a crank is made to stymie the lefty. Boat winches, fishing reels, and even pencil sharpeners are but a few. If you want to see some frustrated people, install the same equipment so it's handy for the southpaw. It tickles me just to think about it. After all the time I've spent doing it their way, it would feel weird to me too.

Like any minority, I think we should be given special consideration. A beauty pageant would be nice; "Miss Lefty America". A couple days before the fishing season starts, set aside days for the southpaw angler. I also think we could use a holiday; since righties always use the left side of the week, we'd take a Friday, preferably during fishing season.

How many left-handed hunting bows grace the racks and shelves? Try to go bowling; the balls are scarce and the shoes hardly ever exist. Even eating out with a group, brings humble pie for the southpaw. He must sit on the end so he don't get in anyone's way. The poor devil is at outcast, and everyone publishes it; "Leave Denny sit over there. He's left-handed, you know!" "Look out for lefty when he swings that fishing rod, he'll hang a treble hook in your ear!" See what I go through?

The lefties have the market cornered in the different view department. A southpaw looks at things in a little different light. He has to, in order to survive. Whenever all the avenues of solution have been explored, look to the leftie for a new batch of roads. To the north paw, they may seem contravene but hear him out. Some people have been downright astonished at some of the ideas I've come up with. Come to think of it, so have I.

Lefties make good trouble-shooters. We're always looking for the reason things aren't working properly. The inventiveness and ingenuity of the southpaw is unequaled. Right-handers make a lot of use of the left side of the brain, southpaws are mostly in their right mind.

Southpaw criminals don't fare nearly as well as their counterparts in law enforcement. They are forced to wear their left-handedness like a tattoo, and that alone diminishes their chances for success. Now you take a lefty criminal in law enforcement; he has a chance. If this paragraph confused you; you are not a lefty.

The next time you do a simple task, change hands. Please wait till you are not in the bathroom. I don't want to be responsible for anything like that.

"The End"

THINGS YOU NEVER SAY

Here is a can of worms that has no bottom. Fish and man have a lot in common in the open mouth department. Neither gets in near as much trouble if he keeps his mouth shut. I've known people who were much more handicapped than any deaf person, simply because they could talk. Poverty, injury, inconvenience, embarrassment, sweat, rejection, and even death can be caused by improper use of the mouth. This tattletale of the mind is the reason leaders seldom ad lib. Someone may think you are an idiot, but he is never sure until you open your mouth.

"Let me pick up the tab this time!" This stunt can easily send you home broke or, at the very least, needy. This is often a ploy to get someone else to argue with you for the bill. In my circles it means you get to pay. Unless you are definitely taking turns, and know what it costs, keep your trap shut. You aren't going to get anything but a thank you from me, because I believe it's impolite to turn down a gift.

"Check it over. Give it whatever it needs. Make it like new." Give these three commands to a shifty mechanic, and I guarantee, he'll be able to take that trip to Europe, he always dreamed of. You better have a drool towel for him and a crying towel for yourself.

Here are some more signs of impending destitution.

"Naw, I don't need an estimate."

"This outboard motor's got a tick in it. It annoys me. Fix it."

"Sorry I broke it. What'll it cost to replace?"

"Sure, you can borrow it. You break it you fix it." "Fine with me."

"Just send me the bill."

"How would you do it?"

"Give me the best one you got."

"I want the works."

"I know it's Christmas day. I need a plumber."

"Move that wall."

"Make me out a bill, you idiot!"

"What is a great boat like this worth, right now?"

I'm sure you have some to add to this, but it don't take long to get depressed making this kind of list.

The injury department is just as nasty as any. "Toss that knife over here." "Throw me that baseball bat." "Flip that hammer to me." "Give me your best shot." "Get out of the way. I'm not afraid." "I can carry more than that." "I'll hold it. You hit it with the mall." "That dog don't look so mean to me!" "Bears are more afraid of me, than I am of them." "I hooked up the tow chain. Take off!" "One more good yank should do it!"

Let's move on to the inconvenience department, it's not so painful. "If you can't find anyone, I'd be glad to help." They will look no further. "I'll do it for nothing!" "What a nice dog! Anytime you need a sitter, let me know." "Sure was nice seeing you! Next year, spend the week at our house." "It's no trouble at all!" "Don't worry, I'll clean it up later!" "Don't hold it in, too much gas could make you feel bad!" Be ready. "Don't take a bath on my account!" "Put the thermostat wherever you want!" "Don't bother to wipe it off your shoes. I don't mind the smell of cat poop in a warm car."

Enough already, on to the embarrassment department. "What ever happened to that old cow you use to take out?" "Oh my gosh, was that me?" "It's all my fault." "I can do that!" "I'll show you how to train that big dog. I'll rub his nose in it." "Who the devil is that ugly thing coming up your front walk?" "Who drew this infantile thing, hanging on your refrigerator?" "Wow, look at that junk-heap! Which car is yours?" "Hey, I thought you put out the dog food already!" Here's some more, on the stove." "Who's that waving at us? What a chunk!" "Holy smoke, what's that smell?" "Did I take your chair? Let me help you up."

The sweat department can be avoided the next time around. "I'll walk, it can't be far." "I'll take the mow, you unload." "Forget the trolling motor, I like to row!" "Stay here, I'll go look for your dog." "You drive, I'll push!"

The rejection department is totally nonexistent if not advertised. "Hand me my little urinal, I gotta take a walk." "What was in that hot dish? I'm really getting a gas buildup." "Do you mind if I belch in here, or should I step outside?" "Good thing I'm not wearing light colored pants. Wow, what a round in the bathroom!" Disgusting ain't it.

The death department is simple. Don't ever say, "Go ahead, shoot!"

"The End"

LET'S GET A BIRD THAT TALKS

A browse through a pet store can lead to future pleasure, anticipation, apprehension, excitement, pain, anger, and in some cases stark terror.

If your life has any other stress factor built in, it is wise to get a pet with a volume control.

The bright green canure seemed so shy and cute when we got him. Hose' was timid and frightened in his new surroundings. It is hard to believe that we were afraid of such a small bird, but I guess it was not knowing what to expect of him. When we put feed and water in his hundred dollar cage, he was bouncing off the walls.

It wasn't very long before the dreaded day came. Someone was going to clean that filthy cage. I was working, so it would not be me. Of course, I do wish a videotape had been made so I could have enjoyed it later. Shirley's rendition of the scene was very good, but to see it would have been great!

Shirley dressed up in heavy clothes, a winter hat, glasses, and thick gloves not unlike falcon handlers use. As she approached the cage, the bird took one look at this creature, and flew into a frenzy. He was surely being attacked.

With locked jaws and fierce determination, Shirley reached into the cage. Feathers clouding the air, blurred her vision as she flailed the entire inside of the cage for her quarry. Hose' finally tired of his game and was nailed in the corner of his cage.

Bird in hand, Shirley looked him in they eye, and squeezed Hose' ever so slightly. Hose' understood who would rule the aviary.

This victory won, Shirley happily shoved him into a grocery bag. She popped in a couple of staples across the top to prevent his escape.

Shirley cleaned the cage till it sparkled. When she returned Hose' to his lodgings he was a different bird. Shirley's victory was complete.

Now that the preliminaries were over, Hose' was coming around. We gained his confidence, and he was actually showing hints of affection. It was a special day when I reached into the cage and he hopped on my finger, instead of biting it. This feathered friend has possibilities.

I bought a couple of books at the pet store, and Hose's training was underway. His home opened to the outside world, and he was in heaven. Hose's wings had been clipped, but he crawled up on his roof, and strutted to his hearts content. I made him a ladder, propped it up to his front door, and quickly he was down, waddling around us as we lounged on the living room floor watching TV.

Our son Steve, lived on the living room floor. Baseball cards, toys, and homework all got their attention from the prone position. It's no wonder that Hose' would be mulling around there too.

Hose' would climb all over him, pull his hair, and nibble on his ears and face. Steve would sometimes grab him, and roll around on the carpet. Ever braver, Hose' soon bestowed his affections on us all.

Our two dogs, Trixie the Pomeranian housedog, and Pokey Joe our collie, were treated in their own special way. Hose' never let his trivial size get in the way of his domination of these canine underlings. Hose' bugged Pokey the most, maybe because she wasn't in the house too often, but most likely because the collie was easy going.

Hose' would chew at Pokey's tail, walk around and bite her lip, then crawl up on her back and clamp onto a furry ear. When Pokey's patience was all used up, Hose' would scurry away, out of range. One time I blocked his escape. Pokey's paw nailed him to the carpet for a satisfying 15 to 20 seconds. It was great!

I suppose you are noticing a little hint of a change in attitude toward this green Aver. Read on.

Hose' was now ready for the next stage in his education. We would teach him to talk. The book said to look him in the eye, and try to get him to repeat what you say. I said "Hello" so many times that I made myself hoarse, Shirley intensely annoyed and the bird merely amused. Soon I just went to the pet store and got a tape that played phrases over and over next to Hose's covered cage. The tape played over and over until someone, very irritated, burned it in the garbage.

Hose' finally learned to talk about the same time he learned how to fly. He'd fly from room to room so he could keep track of everyone. Hose' would land wherever he could find an interesting spot.

Our shoulders and heads became a favorite perching pad. The first time he committed an indiscretion down my back, I thought it was an accident. Now, I don't think so. He dumped on me often, the pig, a couple times right on my head. Then, he'd have the nerve to lean down, say "Hello", and in a flash, snap off one of my shirt buttons.

I was the only one Hose' crapped on, but he used his skills to terrorize visitors. I've seen him fly in low, land on a lady's head, then hang on for dear life, while she screeched and flailed her arms, running wildly around the room. These are the times I miss most.

Shirley's original fear had long since turned to disdain as this messy eater tossed seeds all over the floor. He'd even pull out feathers and throw them around just to make her angry.

Once I'd get him rolled over on his back on the floor, he seemed helpless, as I rolled him from side to side. I'd quit it when it looked like he was enjoying it.

Hose's baths under the kitchen faucet were one of his most entertaining antics. After a while, Shirley was no longer amused to clean up the watery mess.

We even got out of the habit of playing board games. Hose' leaped on the board and scattered play pieces, using his beak to clear the deck, if he felt the center of attention had drifted too far from him.

Before you judge me too harshly for getting rid of one of the family, consider this:

You might want to contemplate what it would feel like, to walk in a house and have something land in you hair. Anyone with a frail heart might suffer <u>the big one</u>, right then and there. If they had just watched a bat movie, the effect could be memorable indeed.

The frightening wail would start low, then begin to rise, finally rising to a pitch that would shatter crystal. I'm almost ashamed to admit, this was also one of the things I liked about him. Shame on me.

He's been torturing some other family for quite some time, though I must admit, I'd like to visit Hose' once in a while.

By Dennis P. Kolb

NIGHT SHIFTER'S GRINDING GEARS

When you know someone who works the night shift, a word to the wise is in order. Give him a wide berth and cut him some slack. If he handles it anything like me, he's wound extra tight. Everyone handles it differently, no one seems to handle it well.

Sleep schedules are erratic, some sleeping its done whenever it works best for each individual. Personally, I sleep as long as I can in the morning, be it 10 a.m. or noon. Then it's back to bed a little in the evening before work. Some barely sleep at all.

At work I've seen and experienced some strange scenes. I've seen those neck snapping 5 a.m. nods, the walking zombies, and the death of all reason when it comes to making sensible decisions. I've found a steer doesn't feel a punch between the eyes nearly so much as me. I've also noticed, shaking it wildly does not help the pain go away.

I've found, a garage door opener doesn't realize when I'm on the night shift. In spite of how many times you press the button, a frozen down door will not open before you smoke the opener. Knowing the outcome does not dissuade the action.

I've found that traffic lights will wait for everyone but me. Flying through the intersection, bottoming the springs on the bump, on the changing light, I sneer to my left. Waiting for his light to change to green, is an officer of the law. He has me dead to rights if he so chooses. As my eyes glue to the rear view mirror, he goes straight ahead. Of course, he must work 11 to 7 too.

I've found myself following slow traffic all through a town. "When we hit the first passing zone, these guys are history." I planned. The opportunity comes. Slingshot into the passing lane and by four, a gravel truck, two cars and a squad car, and accelerating. A %#%#%#%# cop! Oh nooooo!! I can hear flushing money. In instant terror, from near 80 to 55, in behind the semi-trailer ahead and cop car behind.

He's got me. I'm dead meat. What's he waiting for? He's probably getting my life story from my plate number.

For twenty miles, the parade stays the same. I set the cruise on slow. In Stratford, I turn to the south on highway 97. The trooper turns too. Now, he'll nail me. Six more miles. I turn on county trunk 'T'. The state boy goes straight. "Aaagh!"

I've found that a ringing telephone, when sleep won't come, has an accelerating effect on an already bad mood. After about the fifth ring, visions of the underground wire, being ripped out, all the way to the caller's house seemed reasonable to me. When the phone is taken off the hook, it soon gives off a wooooooeeeeooo sound that's nice and calming.

I've found that nature calls me out of bed to the bathroom, regardless of whether I had a drop to drink in 24 hours. If you try to ignore the call, you will be awake as long as you persist in your folly. Once you've gone, you may as well stay up. Gotcha!

If you work 11 to 7, take a look at your hands. Any black fingernails? Bet you got em on 11 to 7. Scars, cuts, and bruises just stick to that shift like a magnet. Any sore part gets knocked around at every turn.

Even the dog knows when I'm on 11 to 7. If she's in a lousy mood, she knows who to pick on. Just as I'm drifting off, she lumbers over to just outside my bedroom window. She makes believe she sees something, and lets fly with her best barking barrage. Right now, I'm standing in the middle of the bed. Then it's my turn to bark, and I can be a lot fiercer than she. I work the night shift!

I've been sleeping soundly, only to be awakened by a variety of disasters;

❖ Shirley was standing there with her fingers wedged tight in the beaters of the mixer. Help! That mixer is now retired.

❖ Seven little pigs out and were running down the driveway. Hence, a new hefty fence.

❖ The neighbor lady hits the train with her car. With all that excitement, out front, who can sleep.

❖ A man from Hewitt, skidded and wrapped his car around my sturdy mailbox. He didn't know whether to be sad or mad. His car had to be lifted off the mailbox with a wrecker, but had the mailbox not stopped his progress, he surely would have been upside down, or worse, in the deep ditch. He may also have smucked the train.

I had installed that post twice. The first time the postman left a note that the height was not correct. It was buried in, and filled with cement to hinder the snowplowers in their little game of mailbox destruction. This is very popular with certain drivers.

❖ A horrendous storm was raging. We were in the basement, I just out of bed. The front door blew open, water coming in! I ran upstairs, barefoot, forced the door shut, and was hurrying back to the basement. I hit the smooth dining room floor. I slipped and went sprawling, amid my howls of pain and Shirley's howls of laughter, almost through the patio door. I quickly gathered my bruised body to the safety of the basement.

❖ "Wake up, there's a skunk outside Get your gun!" The dog was already in high gear when I got to the front window. She grabbed the skunk, snapped its neck, threw it in the air, and it was dead when it hit the ground. It never had a chance to spray. If I had shot it, the place would have stunk for weeks.

❖ "Wake up, there's a water leak in the barn!" I hastily scampered into my clothes, and ran to the barn. We got the source shut off, but there was water everywhere. After Shirley and I cleaned up the mess it was too late to go back to bed. Thank God, she is always there to help me with any dirty job.

❖ "Wake up, we've got cattle loose!"

Please excuse me, I have to go now. I've got to work tonight and I'm starting to upset myself.

By Dennis P. Kolb

SNOW PROBLEM AT ALL

We are going to travel through the winters past as seen through my own sometimes bleary eyes. We will expand on the virtues and drawbacks of the various snow removal equipment I have had the pleasure and misfortune to use during those years.

Shoveling the three hundred foot driveway gave me the kind of calorie burning exercise I could use now, if only there was enough spare time. Of course, a driveway of this size is only shoveled when vehicles no longer have a prayer of getting through. Usually, this did not take long at all.

Pitching snow formed big banks on the side of the driveway. Sometimes even if no snow fell, an ill wind might deposit two feet of snow from the lawn to that vacant space between the two banks.

If this started early in the winter, a man could be just skin and bone by spring. Some days, we were trapped behind the banks, not able to get a vehicle out at all. "There has to be a better way."

By the third winter the Kolb family had a snow blower. It was fitted with electric start, chains, and the necessary power to do almost anything. A machine like this could throw snow out of the way and there would be no banks to fill in between.

It was amazing how quickly I learned the limitations of these machines. Mine did not particularly like the gravel driveway, sometimes shearing one more shear pin that I could find. I laid in a big supply of shear pins only to have the gremlins attack another part.

Flat tires were a daily occurrence until tubes were added. Occasionally the engine would get wet, stop, and I'd have to drag it to the closest point my combined extension cords would reach, to plug in the electric starter.

If the snow banks got hard, the snow blower would try to climb over the hard snow to get at some soft stuff. If I fed it with a shovel it would work fine. If someone drove in the driveway before the snow blower got there, the snow would be packed and unblowable. On a clear day, you could hear my verbal lamenting a long way off, while I shoveled the driveway by hand.

During the times when snow conditions were unbeatable for snow blowing the wind will play some ugly tricks. No matter how bundled up I may be, snow would find its way back, covering me form head to foot. My temper would let go about this time, melting the snow that was driven down my neck. Stand clear when you see a fellow in white blowing snow, and for God's sake don't laugh unless you can run faster than him. Once the snow blowing was mastered, the challenge was gone, and it was sold. I told the buyer all its good points, and was so convincing, I almost didn't let the guy have it.

Next came the snow scoop. It was just a big shovel that slid on the ground. The scoop took as long as the shovel.

Motorized snow removal you can ride on looked like the answer to all our problems, provided this machine would start when it was cold. Our old John Deere 'A' was not in new repair, so it was not in a position to challenge for the task at hand.

We found a fine International Farmall 544 that would fill the bill. It had over fifty horsepower, power steering, and was smooth as silk. I scoured the implement lots and found an old loader in our price range. Our price range was beginning to match all that our credit could handle. The old loader had a manure bucket and an eight foot blade that angled to plow snow. To save money, I would put it on the tractor myself. "Heck, how tough can it be?" Two weeks later, we were snowed in so deep we had to hire an end loader to dig out the snow in the yard. Soon after this, the loader was completely installed, and I was ready to go.

I was really excited the next time it snowed. It didn't take long to realize tire chains were a necessity. Next, I strapped two fifty five gallon drums on the back, filled them with water, and let them freeze. Now, we had traction. A windbreaker, from my uncle Mitch, was added too when I found out just how cold it is, with very little wind, sitting atop the tractor.

I plowed in the lowest gear to hold down welding costs on the loader. By moving slow, large banks formed on the sides, and some buildup of snow on the driveway. By late winter, the packed snow was about six to eight inches thick on the driveway. This was okay until the snow started to melt in the spring.

As the snow melted, deep ruts formed in the driveway, making it quite an adventure to get out for a few days, with anything but a four wheel drive.

This was unacceptable, we would have to throw some more money at the problem. We needed an all hydraulic loader, and this time we would have it put on where we bought it.

I watched the mechanics install the new used loader. Judging from the language and use of the cutting torch, I figured we made a good decision this time. I knew how to use the language, but I didn't have a torch.

The loader was heavily built and all that was needed was a snow bucket to match. Bauer Manufacturing built us a bucket. We found a cab that would work, and had it installed. With this setup, we could even make back some of the money we spent. It would take an accountant to figure how many years we would have to use the tractor, to justify the final cost, but it was comforting to know that all our troubles were over.

As time soon proved, even the best equipment can go astray, but that is another story.

The End

GOTCHA!

On the journey through the briar patches of life, I've become aware that, seemingly inanimate objects have a sadistic sense of humor. I've been attacked by objects that seem as lifeless as the dried remains on last years fishing hooks. These blanketies are allowed to come alive long enough to assault me and snigger about it.

Just last night, and old heavy ugly-looking door came to life and nailed my gesturing finger on my right hand. It was waiting for me and put up a good tussle before I yanked it open. The door was setting me up. Before I got there, it had already hidden its doorknob somewhere. After I got through it's opening, it waited for me to close it. I fell into its wretched trap. I grabbed the door edge to pull it after me.

On cue, the door attacked! Woommph! "Aaiiiigh!"

I could hear the door's guttural cackling even over my vile name-calling, as I danced and romped in pain, trying to hold my flailing paw still, long enough to survey the damage. The door let go an audible high-pitched squeal when the blood started spraying the floor. I tried to keep my hand high to stop my strong heart from pumping me dry, while I worked on the second stanza of my pain-song.

Nature had been kind enough to pop the finger like a ripe grape to take the pressure off. Only God knows how much it would have hurt under pressure. That blasted door would still be grinning. The pain that spewed out of that finger could have filled a 55 gallon drum.

I wrestled the hand down where I could look at the damage. I wouldn't be typing with this sucker for a while. The finger and hand got a washing before I could find out where the sap was coming from.

I left a trail to the sink, a blind hyena could follow. After the cold water washed away the gore, I could see it was a three band-aid-er. I spent the next 45 minutes hunting for three band-aids.

Have you ever noticed how the bandages can't be removed from the package when you have a wound. These simple cut-coverers never tire of this one sick joke. The little string will not rip the package open. It just pulls out straight and wags its tail at you. The ignorant blankity-blank-of-a-blank.

When I was finally bandaged up, there was no time to inflict any serious revenge on the door. I did inflict enough verbal abuse on it to make a train take a dirt road, however. It didn't seem to phase it.

Some inanimate objects are satisfied to merely fester an injury already inflicted. So it was as I went through the day with the tender finger. It seemed like I had a grapefruit where the finger should be. Car doors, steering wheels, eating utensils, and even remote controls, took their turn battering the door's victim. Each of these nit-pickers got their ears full as they sought to extend my discomfort.

Once I get this thing healed up I'm not going to forget those sadistic swipes. Every chance I get I'm going to inflict a little pain of my own. A kick here, a punch there; I'll get em. Nothing is going to attack me and get off scott-free. The biggest problem with revenge on an inanimate object is never knowing when you've got them off-guard.

A lot of people I've talked to use the same method to get under the skin of these dealers of pain. When one object gives them crap, another object takes the heat. One time I busted a steering wheel when an engine wouldn't start. It felt great! The next time an adjustable wrench crunches your knuckles, slam a door in my honor. Get the idea? Tit for tat.

Some people get this method of revenge turned around. I've had it backfire on me, too. Let's say something attacks my wife, in the kitchen. There have many times when I, an innocent bystander, have taken the heat instead of the real blankity culprit.

Sometimes a big inanimate object can inflict enough fear in a victim, to make a corpse run for cover. A tree shadow, a little wind, and the fluttering wings of a bat have been known to fill a man's pants with solids, liquids, or both.

Be on your guard and keep your head. Tomorrow is a new day.

"The End"

FREE WOOD AND WOOD STOVES

ack in the 70s when the energy crunch laid siege on us, we counter-attacked. Nobody would hold our furnace for ransom. We'd heat our home with some of the free wood that's everywhere around us, just for the taking. Maybe these Arabs don't know who they're dealing with. A little lesson is in order.

We were required to gather and buy some equipment to gather and burn the free wood. Of course, this equipment would pay for itself in no time at all. After all, the free wood was close enough. It sure was going to be our lucky day when we would be fortunate enough to be the recipient of free heat. What would we do with all the extra cash?

First of all, we needed a stove to burn the free wood in. The stove had to meet the requirements of the insurance company. We found a stove that exceeded the requirements and the amount we had intended to spend. It had an automatic damper and looked like a short version of the oil-burner that stood in our living room when I was a kid. It was a handsome stove.

By the time the new stove was installed, it cost as much as a years supply of heating oil. Undaunted, we burned lumber scraps and saved money. The basement was warm as toast, and in no time at all. A little of the heat came upstairs, too. The floors were nice and warm. Soon our supply of lumber was depleted. We would have to gather some of that free wood.

I bought a bow saw and an ax. We started making wood. I quickly learned that more heat was being generated making the wood, than we would ever get out of it. We would need to invest in a chain saw. It was becoming apparent that I was using my pocketbook a lot more than my brain to solve these continuing challenges. My mood skyrocketed when I realized all these wood-making costs would be deductible if I started selling all the excess wood I was going to make. With this in mind, I went to Willie's Chain Saw Service.

The chainsaw, sharpener, file, extra chain, oil to mix with the gas, gas, and bar chain oil cost was well over half a year's heating oil. The saw was the smallest one he could sell me, that had any kind of life span. The big saws were out of reach of my pocket book even if I reached clear down inside my pants, to my ankle. Willie equipped me well.

I already owned a pickup so I was ready to start making free wood. I gathered all the new tools into the truck and drove to the first free tree I could find. It wouldn't be long now. Free heat was a close reality.

It's a good thing the bow saw and ax were among the tools in the truck. In fact, a couple more tools might have come in handy to get the wedged chain saw out of the log. By the time I sawed and chopped enough wood away to free the saw, I was pretty well tired out. It was better to go home and rest up for tomorrow.

Tomorrow arrived early the next morning amid grunts, groans, and sore muscles. Nursing my coffee and body, I pored over a catalog of wood-making accessories. They were all there, dollar signs and all. Rather than buy all the tools made, I confided in some fellows who make wood for a living. Looking around their place, I noticed that these guys didn't flaunt their wealth. I liked that. I bought the equipment they suggested. The second year's heating fuel cost was history by days end. Oh, but the deductions.

The next time out I didn't quit till the truck was full of free wood. There was an ever-so-slight problem. Three fourths of the load would not fit into the stove. The double-bit ax wasn't made to split wood. Neither was I, come to think of it. At any rate, I bought a new mall, a splitting mall, and a splitting wedge.

I started splitting the tough pith Elm chunks. After I got into the third chunk, things came to an impasse. The wedge and the splitting mall were stuck tight in the pith Elm chunk. I ran and bought two more wedges. I got them stuck too. Anyone within earshot knew things were not going well.

In desperation, I got out the chainsaw. Except for ruining one of the chains on a wedge, the chunk was split without further ado. When I had a stack of wood that took up twice the space of the fuel oil barrel, I quit. Since I used two tanks of heating oil the winter before, that should just about do it.

The basement was warm. But we spent all our time upstairs where it was chilly. I cut a couple holes in the floor to let the heat come up where we needed it. By the time the wood ran out, the cold days of December were upon us.

When spring arrived, the challenges ahead were clear. First of all, I would need a lot more wood to last through the winter. Secondly, I had to find a way to get more of the heat upstairs, from the stove. Thirdly, I would have to cut down dead pith Elm's still standing, to get enough free wood. The splitting part bothered me, but first things first.

By the end of the summer we made twenty cords of wood, I learned to fell trees (that's another story), and the stove had a bonnet to direct the heat upstairs. Fifteen cords of wood needed to be split.

After splitting three cords by hand, it was obvious time was not on my side.

I rented an engine-driven hydraulic wood splitter. All the wood was split and piled by days end. We had twenty cords of free wood ready to burn.

The wood rack I built in the basement held five cords. When that was burned, we spent the rest of the winter digging the needed free wood out of the snow banks and hauling it by wheelbarrow on shoveled paths to the basement window.

When the financial challenge wore off, I bought a bigger saw and a better stove. Next we bought eight-foot lengths of wood by the semi load, and half-interest in a splitter. Lately, I've been buying the wood ready to burn.

All the free wood is finally burned up.

"The End"

TRACTORS N' HAY

My motorized haying career began early in life. My first tractor driving job took me aboard a shiny yellow-orange Minneapolis Moline owned by my uncle Mitch. It had a hand clutch and was almost new. It was a beauty.

I had wandered over to my uncle's place that day during my bicycle travels. When Mitch asked if I'd like to drive for him, I jumped at the chance. Make-believe driving a stationary 37 Chevy at home in the garage just wasn't the same. This was the real thing!

Out in the field, Mitch started the engine and showed me the tractor controls. He told me what I needed to know about while he was on the wagon spreading the loose hay as it came off the hay loader. When he was ready, all I had to do was engage the hand clutch and we would be on our way. To stop, I was to disengage the clutch or shut off the ignition switch. I could handle that.

We were ready. The engaging of the clutch was easy. Once done, all I had to do was keep the front tires on the windrow. It was great driving around the field with all that power under my command. Mitch was a young man, and he didn't yell for me to stop until we had almost half a load.

Off the seat and in back on the hand clutch lever, I yanked on it with both hands. Try as I might, I couldn't muster the oomph required to pull it back. I was forced to turn off the ignition switch instead. It was a personal defeat having to resort to the switch. Mitch had to come down off the load to disengage the clutch and restart the tractor.

As the load got bigger we had to stop a few more times. Each time I tried to yank the clutch out without success. Each time Mitch had to climb down, pull it back, and restart the engine.

When the load was nearly full we had to stop again. This time Mitch came up with a great idea. He had me turn on the ignition with the clutch still engaged. Then he had me push the starter button. The tractor started and we were off again at the same time.

I don't remember how many loads we hauled. I do remember the best job to have while making hay is aboard the tractor.

It's been over thirty five years but I still remember the good pork chops we had for supper. I remember how good ketchup makes them taste. I'd never seen that before. Mitch put ketchup on his pork chops. So did I. It was great!

Baling hay became the norm as soon as it hit the fields. At first there was a lot of hiring of baling crews and the bales were very heavy. It could possibly be that as I got older I could lift a lot more. Lately the bales seem to be getting heavier again.

After helping my brother, Vernie, for a couple of haying seasons, I decided I sort of enjoyed this farming thing. Vernie's baler was a temperamental misfit. For two years in a row, we used Mitch's fine baler. It was a John Deere 14T model. It never gave any trouble at all. I talked my wife into letting me buy one just like it. I assured her it would bring us unbelievable revenues helping Vernie and selling hay on our own.

We bought a John Deere "A" tractor and a new hay wagon at the same time we bought the baler. Mitch gave us an old side rake. We were in business.

The baler worked almost flawlessly through the years I've owned it. With regular maintenance, good twine, and grease it has lasted and performed well. The tractors, on the other hand, had personalities as varied as their number.

At first we used the "A" on the baler. It had good power but if the hay was heavy the ground speed could not be slowed without slowing the speed of the baler. Under normal conditions, this was not a problem. The outside windrow was not a normal condition. It was two windrows in one and a formable challenge.

We were baling in a well endowed field, Shirley was my driver, when this dilemma first came up. Leave it to a wife to shake one to reality.

"What are you going to do on the outside row?" Shirley asked.

Till now I'd kept my mouth shut for lack of an answer. Now I would have to make a stab at a solution.

"I guess we'll go at it wide open in low gear until the tractor chokes or we shear a pin." I heard myself say.

It seemed reasonable to me, but Shirley shook her head in disgust at the idea. She would have traded in her driving gloves in a flash if there were another driver. I assured her that the old Johnny Popper could handle it, probably. Shirley was not convinced but she does not give up just because she believes the odds are too great.

We hooked on an empty wagon and headed toward our windrow of windrows. The closer we got the bigger it looked. This could get ugly!

A safe distance away, Shirley stopped to set the controls. She engaged the power take-off and put the tractor in gear number one. She engaged the hand clutch and gave the Johnny full throttle.

We hit the windrow on the run. The bales were coming so fast I had to throw some of them back on the field just to have a chance at keeping up. Shirley kept looking back at me as the Johnny's pops were getting farther apart as it waded into the heavy windrow. To her dismay I waved her on as bale after bale churned through the 14T. I was impressed!

We were three quarter of the way around the field and the engine pops were an eternity apart with their explosions of compressed power.

"Hang in there, Johnny!"

The granddaddy slug of hay went into the mouth of the "T". In one fell swoop, the Johnny choked and every pin sheared on the "T". Quiet.

Shirley started expressing her heated dissatisfaction as she climbed down off the Johnny. I was definitely to blame for the stress inflicted on her and she told me so in no uncertain terms.

As for me, I was kind of glad it finally stopped. I had over half a load of hay and twenty or so bales laying on the field, that I hadn't been able to handle.

It took half an hour to clean the ball of hay out of the baler. It took another half and hour changing shear-pins and gathering bales. I was actually avoiding the rest of the windrow as long as possible.

By thinning out the rest of the windrow with a fork we got through the rest of it without further incident.

We borrowed my brother's Allis Chalmers to bale with whenever we could get it, after that. The W-D had a little less power, but two clutches. If the hay got thick, we could slow down the tractor without slowing the baler speed. It worked great, but we needed a tractor of our own.

We bought a Farmall 544. It had 52 horse power and a torque amplifier. When the going got tough, a lever was pulled and the red machine reached back and gave you whatever you needed to power through the heaviest windrow.

In the years since, we have graduated from making thousands of bales to making hundreds instead. We enjoy the slower pace but would not be happy to quit altogether. The animals we keep are a reason to get going on a nasty day and a built-in excuse at a boring party.

"The End"

ALMOST READY TO SELL

Summer was here and everyone was asking when I would have some more beef to sell. Usually, we like to buy small calves and raise them until we can't afford to feed them anymore. We then sell the beef.

I didn't have any calves right then and needed something to sell. I could see a huge profit looming off in the distance somewhere. Why put all that feed into them? Why have them for such a long time? The faster they are sold, the more money you can make! Such an opportunity! Why hadn't I thought of it before? Everyone who knew about it was keeping all that profit to themselves. I'll buy some cattle that are almost ready to sell, feed them for about three moths, and take the profit on the way to the bank.

I scoured the newspapers for about a week before the lucky break came. A fellow had six head to sell. It was less than ten miles away.

Before buying anything, I would check things out thoroughly. No one was going to pull anything on this shrewd trader and haggler. All sides will be looked at, all precautions taken, and the lowest price paid. Everyone will marvel at my business sense and maybe even look me up for advice.

I drove to the fellow's farm. He had a small cow-calf operation, with a lot of pasture that went a ways back into the swamp. He used single wire electric fence to keep them in. I could hardly hold back my excitement. They were so calm. I never had any animals I could keep in with a single wire electric fence. I used four foot high woven wire, with electrified barbed wire on top and in front, so they wouldn't mash it down. This was great!

He said he had fed them a little hay on the side, but otherwise just pasture. The animals all weighed about six hundred pounds or so. He had six ready to go. He even had a place to load them. It just could not be any easier. Wow, feed these guys for about two months and sell em' for beef! Coyly, I told him the price wasn't too bad, but I'd have to think about it.

I went right home and asked Shirley if she would be willing to help take care some cattle for about two months. "You're sure they're not wild?" "No way, he's got one wire electric fence." "You're sure you can get rid of all the beef?" "Yeah, I'll be lucky to have enough to go around." "Remember the Scotch Highland." I quickly turned away so she couldn't see my face turn white like that. "Well O.K. if you think you know what you're doing." Boy, I never expected that. Full approval with no questions asked.

On the way to the bank, I stopped to see Bratt Mitten. If the bank lent me the money, I'd need the trailer to haul the cattle home.

"Did ya find some more Scotch Highlanders? heh heh heh." "No way, this time I found some they can keep in with a one wire electric fence." I could tell he was impressed, but he cackled a lot longer than was necessary. I remember a couple times things weren't so darn funny for him.

The bank approved the loan, but he gave me that kind of look that lets you read minds. He was thinking, "Good thing this joker has a good job", as he inked the deal.

I raced home and called the farmer to make sure all six cattle were still there. "Sure, I'll get em ready," he said.

Bratt was still chuckling over his earlier smart remark when I picked up the trailer. I let it pass cause the whole good deal would eventually speak for itself. I was on my way to financial freedom this time for sure.

The man was ready for me when I pulled into the yard. The trailer backed easily up to the chute. "How many in this load?" "Oh heck, I may as well do it in one trip." "That's quite a load, I don't know if you want to do that," he said. "Let's put them in there and we'll see," I said with assurance. No problem!

It felt like quite a load, as we were driving out. Bratt had hauled seven ponies back from Iowa in this trailer, so why worry? In half a mile, we were on the highway.

Not too far down the road, I heard some scraping. We pulled over on the shoulder of the road and stopped right away. The rubbing tires on one side were smoking. Maybe we've got too big a load. We managed to limp back to the guy's farm, eat a little crow, and let three off. Since he had my money, he was kind enough to keep his mouth shut.

We made the two lighter trips with no incident, cleaned out the trailer, and took it back.

I put out hay and feed for the steers. They ate the hay but didn't know what the feed was. Oh well, they will learn soon enough. After dark, the cattle seemed to be getting a little restless. We went to bed.

During the night, the new steers started mooing and bellowing a little. Toward morning, it seemed quite loud. Shirley looked out the window. "You better get up. The cattle are out!" she yelled. "Oh no!" I wailed. I got outside just in time, to see one sail over the four foot high fence. They were walking around in the yard just bellowing. Now, what's wrong? They kept getting more upset and were starting to move around. It seemed like they were looking for something. Things were not going well. Bratt would really enjoy this. Another couple of bellers and the rest of them cleared the fence. I just followed them around not knowing what to do.

The animals were roaming around in a bunch, a couple hundred yards, behind the buildings. Maybe the banker was right.

Bill Scherr showed up about this time and suggested I open up the rear shed door. He sure thought the situation was a lot funnier than I did. Of course, it wasn't his money. Things like that make a big difference. Somehow we got five of them to go in the right direction and locked them in the barn. The other steer bolted and headed for a herd of cows he saw half a mile away.

Bill knew what was wrong right away. "They miss their mothers, they haven't been weaned", he chuckled. "Leave them in the barn a couple days. They'll be okay."

Just to be sure, I bought the hottest fencer I could find.

Late that night, Bratt was being paid back for chiding me about the cattle. It was hot, so he had his bedroom window open to the east. He was serenaded all night long by a bellowing mournful steer. He was a little hostile the next day, himself.

The steer finally followed the farmers' cows into the barn where he caught him.

Prices went up so fast that year, nobody had any money to buy beef. I ended up feeding them all winter and losing money in the spring.

So goes another brilliant idea, but I've got another one, a sure-fire one brewing.

"The End"

BEES ALIVE

The nice warm September day seemed just right to haul a little manure. I hadn't used the old spreader for a while, so I would check for a weak spots and grease the moving parts. The manure spreader had a lot of makeshift parts that didn't resemble the original pieces at all. I prided myself when my idea made it work better at little or no cost. Junk is cheap. It had given me fifteen years and was borderline junk when I bought it from Ray Felton for one hundred twenty five bucks. Some parts didn't get replaced. If they didn't look necessary or still had a couple hours life expectancy, I'd forget it. "If it ain't broke, don't fix it!"

The pile of rotted manure stood just off the road, the manure spreader parked in front of it, just off the driveway. It brightened up the front lawn nicely.

I checked the fuel level in the Oliver 77. This tractor didn't come with a gas gauge so I made a stick with graduated marking on to determine the fuel level. The stick revealed very little gas left in the tank. "Oh boy, almost empty, but maybe just enough to move the spreader up to the shop," I thought, "and maybe find that gas leak."

"Ah," I thought, "on days like this it's great to be alive. The trees are just starting to turn and my tractor is running great!" As I was hooking up the hitch to the spreader I noticed kind of a buzzing sound. "Hmm, What's that?"

The jack was just up when the bees started working around me. I do not like bees, and I was doing some flying of my own. At thirty yards and out of breath, I stopped to survey the situation and catch my breath.

The tractor was running, blocking the driveway, almost out of gas, and hooked to a bee infested manure spreader. I was pacing back and forth just out of bee range, waiting for a lull in the bee activity, trying to think of something. I had to get the tractor out of there before it ran out of gas. It would be a mile walk for a can of gas, to say nothing of the chance of smart remarks when you arrive on foot with an empty gas can.

The tractor noise was aggravating the bees into a frenzy. The situation was deteriorating quickly.

In thoughtless 11 to 7 bravery, I ran to the tractor, jumped on, and drove away flailing my arms in a flurry of profanity. In the three hundred feet to my destination, I was stung three times and had used up most of the nasty words I knew. I finally shut off the tractor and hit the ground running.

While I licked my wounds, Shirley went to town to get some bug spray for the wasps. By the time Shirley returned, I was recovered enough to spray some revenge on my attackers.

I soaked the nest with bug spray until the purr of the wasps died off. "Well," I thought, "That's just about enough for today."

Now it was about two P.M. and the mail would be here soon. I was looking over my handy work when I saw Matt Pankratz coming along delivering his mail. This was his last year before retirement.

You could set your watch by him. I hoped his replacement would be as good as Matt, or Ray Manlick before him.

He slowed up, so I knew Matt would stop. Matt stopped, but took off almost immediately. Gravel was flying and both wheels spinning as he left the mailbox. "Boy, he's in a hurry today!" I thought.

All the sudden, he slammed on the brakes, bailed out of his car, and was running around the road, yelling and swatting the air! Somehow the scene looked familiar.

I hustled out to the road to see what the trouble was. "There's a bunch of bees in the damn mail box!", he said. "I got nailed a couple times and there are some more in the car!"

I was doubled with laughter, while Matt tired to explain how the wasps swarmed into the car when he opened the mailbox. I was enjoying myself too much to hear it all. I was usually the laughee, so this was great!

"Shut up Kolb, it isn't funny!" Matt wailed. After he calmed down, I told Matt the manure spreader story. Matt's cackling over the story took the sting out of my own enjoyment in a hurry. I should never have told him.

I sprayed out the mailbox before the wasps made it a home.

The next day I watched by the window, with binoculars, as Matt snuck up on the mailbox. It was great! I could see the muscles tense in his face, as he snapped it open and shut, barely getting the mail in.

The next day I put the flag up, to mail an unnecessary letter, just to watch the wary mailman flinch.

"Ah, the county life has its little everyday pleasures!"

By Dennis P. Kolb

IMPRACTICAL JOKES

Over the years I have been associated with people who have a suspect sense of humor. Their antics are limited only by their imaginations. Terrorists could learn from them. Some of the devices they use have a definite terrorist air about them. Back in my Dad's time, the pranks were illusionary or merely distasteful, or kept secret.

I've heard tell how they dealt with one fellow who used his horse as a homing pigeon. For an evening of liquid refreshment, this fellow had an advance plan. He'd leave his car home since he'd be in no condition to drive at closing time. He used a horse and buggy for his drinking transportation, instead. Traffic was sparse so this worked quite well.

At closing time, he'd either walk, crawl, or be carried to his buggy. As soon as the horse was untied, he'd go home without any guidance from his passenger. This was a perfect setup.

A couple of the patrons of the Rock Inn devised a way to make his trip more interesting. They swapped the wheels on the buggy. They put the larger wheels on the front and the smaller ones on the back. That night he rode uphill all the way home.

Halloween tricks were devised from whatever was handy. A little gravel inside the hubcaps or a little Limburger cheese on the manifold was very effective. Limburger gets ripe in a hurry when it's heated.

Outhouses were a favorite target too, until they got scarce. Some were tipped over so often, the owners put hinges on one side so they would be easier to reset. My uncle Mitch used reinforcement to deter the pranksters. He ended up with a nice rear bumper from an unsuccessful Chevy owner.

Mitch stayed up to watch the yearly tradition broken. The Chevy owner may have retrieved his bumper and chain if Mitch had not turned on a light to send him scurrying away. Mitch thought it was a great show. On the other hand, Scutter had to buy a new bumper and chain.

Some say, working the night shift makes people sadistic and dangerous. I say, it has to be in their nature beforehand; the night shift just makes it bloom.

This little incident happened on the night shift on opening day of deer season. Spence, Noel, and Gary were sitting in the 8 X 10 booth checking their equipment for the hunt. Gary was to be the butt of the prank. The prank's main ingredients were a rifle, a spent shell, and an M-80 fire cracker.

Gary's feet were on the desk and his fingers were locked behind his head as he contemplated the hunt. His thoughts were disrupted occasionally by the banter from the other pair.

The silence was broken by a deafening blast as Spence ejected the spent shell from his rifle. Gary's reaction was strong and immediate. He unleashed a stunning explosion of profanity as he picked himself off the floor, using the Lord's name in vain a couple of times and ending with the word fool.

The other two had no idea how much noise an M-80 makes in a closed space. It could have been the end, in a hurry, if any of the three would have had a bad ticker.

All the years I worked at the power plant, the pranks were worked in the same category; fear. I must admit; I did participate a couple of times. I was not a habitual prankster but sometimes I couldn't help it. There were a couple fellow Viet Nam vets who tended to be a bit jumpy. It probably had nothing to do with the war. It could have been something they drank. It was warned that some of the booze could make you go blind. I believe it. I saw quite a few sailors and marines who couldn't see where they were going, especially in Olongapo. I had a couple squashed fingers to prove it.

Let's get back to the fear games. My favorite was one performed on Paul Jantz in the elevator. Just per chance, I saw him walking toward the elevator in deep thought. The elevator was on my floor, giving me a chance to hop aboard. I waited. Sure enough, Paul called the elevator.

When Paul is in deep thought he is oblivious to the world around him; so it was this time. I stood quietly in the rear of the 4X6 foot elevator. Paul never saw me. He was looking at the floor selector buttons as the door closed. He finally decided where he wanted to go. Just as he pushed the button, I touched his shoulder and bid him a soft "hello". His panic was instantaneous. I was laughing much too hard to feel half the blows he pummeled me with, before the elevator stopped again. He owed me.

The elevator was used many times as terrorists laid in wait for the occupant to emerge.

The most ingenious elevator trick goes to Mike Milkey. He climbed through the ceiling trap door in the elevator with a twenty foot piece of cable and waited for his victim. His victim arrived. After his victim selected his destination, Mike started feeding the piece of cable through the open trap door in the elevator ceiling. The occupant stared in terror as the cable was coiling on the floor in front of him. His scream culminated the prank as the other end of the cable hit the floor. The cackling from above was never forgiven. There was an ongoing war till management closed the place down. No other place I've worked had so many sadists in one spot.

Working at Land O Lakes in Spencer, Wisconsin was mildly amusing, however.

I watched, one day, as Herman took his cheese samples for the lab. His tool took core samples from the 55 gallon barrels of cheese. These samples were put in jars and labeled for later analysis. Herman had about a dozen samples to get.

I saw something strange developing about the two barrels behind Herman. Brunel Wunrow was opening the bottles and eating the samples almost as quickly as Herman was filling the bottles, ahead of him. Herman never noticed what was happening as he walked past Brunel to get some more sample bottles.

When Herman returned from the lab, all the bottles were empty. He looked confused, but he took all the samples again, without a word. Brunel never even smiled. I would soon learn more of Brunel's strange sense of humor. Brunel was a low grade criminal. He stole chickens and other strange things. The cops were always watching Brunel; he didn't like it.

One day a squad was following Brunel just a little too close. He mashed on his brakes and took the hit. By the time the officers got out, he was clutching his neck, yelling "whiplash". He was even arrogant enough to try to sue them.

One morning Brunel came to work all scratched up. I asked him what had happened. "The stupid idiot dragged me into the ditch", he said. This, I had to hear.

He was trying to help a friend of his get his car started. The car had an automatic transmission. Brunel figured if they could get it up to about 60 miles an hour in neutral, he could drop the selector to drive and start it like a stick-shift.

Brunel was in the tow vehicle on the highway described as having slippery spots and stretches. As Brunel reached 55 miles an hour, the fellow in tow became frightened out of his wits, and took the ditch. Since Brunel was chained to him, Brunel suffered the same fate. To my surprise, Brunel enjoyed my amusement in the situation. He was a strange fellow.

"The End"

THE PONY HUSTLE

It's early November in Wisconsin and yours truly, Dennis Kolb, gets another memorable lesson in animal behavior.

I acquired a pair of ponies free, from Bratt Mitten, I thought would make a nice team. The team idea quickly went down the tubes when Brownie grew about six inches taller than Diamond. There was still a chance one pony could pull a cart, if I could ever afford one to pull.

When the weather was nice, the ponies were tied out on the lawn to serve as a lawnmower and fertilizer producer. The ponies thought tipping their water pail was fun. Watching me retrieve and fill the pails seemed to amuse them.

Even tied in their stalls, the ponies would get into trouble. They would chew off the rope and wander around using the whole barn for a bathroom. I was beginning to see why Bratt had so freely parted with them.

This November day someone unknown had left open the barn door. Brownie and Diamond were tied in their stalls. Diamond chewed through his rope and found his freedom. When I spotted him in the yard I called him a lot of things, not one of them even close to the gem the pony was named after.

The chase was on. I chased the wily pony all around the yard for a while. Soon the pony got tired of the same scenery and decided to test my endurance. Shirley happened to glance out the window as we headed across the field. I lasted almost half a mile before I was wheezing and gasping for breath. The anger had really helped keep up the pace for a long time.

When Diamond noticed I was recharging, he quickly stopped so he wouldn't get too far ahead. This was a fun game! As I walked toward him, Diamond kept just ahead of me. I felt my strength coming back as I inched ever closer. Just eight feet behind, I bolted into a sprint an Olympic contender would be proud of. Diamond kept eight feet ahead until I was aired out once more. With my hands on my knees, I coughed and choked while my breath came back again. I thought I could hear a distinct horse laugh just ahead. This chase and choke routine went on for almost an hour before we ended up in the yard again.

Shirley knows just about how long my fuse is so she was just coming out of the house. Sometimes I had to be real careful when I needed her to help me. At the first display of off color language, she was gone and would not return. This happened even though I never have directed my onslaught at her.

Now, puffing and coughing, I was stomping toward the house. "Where are you going?", Shirley asked. "I'm getting the gun," I snarled. "Let's see if that S.O.B. can outrun a Winchester!" Shirley grumbled something and kept on walking.

I looked around just in time to see Shirley walk to the pony, take it by the halter, and lead it into the barn. I proceeded directly to the telephone and called fellow worker, Floyd Stugut. "How would you like two FREE ponies?"

In two days Floyd picked up the ponies.

It did not take long before Floyd had some stories of his own for me to enjoy. It seems anytime you get something for nothing, it costs you more than you can comfortably afford. At least, it happens that way for me.

"The End"

LAWN MOWERS ON THE NIGHT SHIFT

Lawnmowers bother night shift workers to no end. It does not make a difference whether he's using it or not. Just listening to one running, while lying in bed, can produce enough emotions to make a consulting psychiatrist leap with delight.

We will travel through some of the challenges encountered when dealing with these vehicles of vengeance.

❖ The bone jarring ride. A dry summer, and an uneven lawn, can punish your posterior to the point of irreparable injury.

The seat can be cushioned, sometimes, but rarely before it has provoked its rider to profanity.

❖ A lethal golf ball, caught with the blade, can send window replacement costs through the roof. I wish my driver could send a golf ball that straight. The lawn mower also leaves a nasty gash, especially, on the balls that are favorites. Ricochet a golf ball off a tree, and you've opened up scads of possibilities.

❖ Dog doodoo has a way of being in the wrong place, during an otherwise uneventful chore. Being sprayed with, or stepping in, this nasty stuff has the same effect. For the 11 to 7 worker, the effect is immediate, and sometimes educational as well.

❖ Things left lying on the lawn can be a source of escalating annoyance. Toys, bones, clothes, and tools, park in front of the lawnmower at every opportunity. I hate to admit it, but, I've disregarded, and run over, stuff, I thought, wouldn't hurt the lawnmower. These hateful feelings are common to the nightshift.

❖ Branches and bushes, have been known to, bodily attack an innocent lawnmower operator. I've seen them knock off hats, inflict scrapes and scratches, and in severe cases, put the pilot sprawling on the ground. These are trying times, and pruning can be rapid and drastic. Whole trees and bushes have been removed, in one fell swoop, in the most extreme cases.

❖ Mowing hills and ditches can be fun whether riding or walking. These should be avoided, completely, if at all possible on 11 to 7. Injuries can be permanent and disabling. At least follow all known precautions to the letter. This particular challenge is one for serious consideration.

❖ Running out of gas is a sure bet as you near the fartherest point from the gas can. On this shift, the gas can, will most likely, be empty. You can tell what shift the guy is on by his reaction to the empty can. If he flails his arms in a whirlwind of profanity, he's on the graveyard shift.

❖ The noise of the engine can get more annoying with each round. You will never see a man, working the night shift, use a lawnmower without a muffler. This would create just enough extra stress to put him over the edge. The noise of a lawnmower, however bothers those trying to sleep, whether the machine has a muffler, or not. Anyone operating a mower within earshot of a guy or a gal, trying to sleep, runs the risk of being throttled for his folly.

❖ A part may fall off or fail, usually leaving the mower stranded, with about three and a half minutes of mowing left. This too, happens as you near the farthest point from your tools. Searching for the lost parts will only annoy you more. Just walk away, or get ready to verbalize your opinion of the situation. Do check the area, for small children, before you let go.

❖ Have you ever noticed how quickly the kidneys beg to be relieved, as soon as you start mowing lawn. I've seen actual beads of sweat form on those stubborn enough to ignore the maddening call of nature.

❖ Rocks and roots only attack a newly sharpened blade. A dull blade will pass over these obstacles, untouched, every time. I think rocks wait, just below the surface, for me to sharpen the blade. Then they pop up, and take out a chunk of metal, the first chance they get.

❖ An innocent looking puddle, not avoided, can inflict enough discomfort to release pent up hostilities, frustrations, and words so distasteful, it almost makes me blush. Stalled in the middle of a puddle, pondering your alternatives, quickly, reminds you of how few alternatives there are, in a situation like this.

❖ I've even had days, of overwhelming stress, when just waiting for these things to happen, spoiled an otherwise beautiful day.

Now, that I've got myself all worked up, I think I'll go lie down.

By Dennis P. Kolb

DOIN TWO MAN JOBS ALONE

The two man job has been a character builder down through the ages. These jobs can be handled by one man if he has a little guts, sprinkled with outright madness. Character and vocabulary are usually built at the same time.

There have been times I looked for two man jobs to do, just for the fun of it. The risk and danger are addicting, somehow. The more necessary the task is, the more dangerous it becomes. Avoid necessary tasks like a chuckhole, if pain is not your fancy.

Try backing a pickup to the exact spot you need to hook up that heavy trailer. I have yet to find a solution that don't involve buying something. If you buy a solution, you have not played by the rules. If you cobble something up, the rules have not been broken. The risk factor has been increased. If you work the night shift, I'm afraid, you can expect disaster. You might want to set up a video camera to show the survivors how you did yourself in. Who knows, the tape might pay for the funeral.

I usually have half a dozen two man jobs going at one time. Some of these jobs are best if they are not rushed. The more time spent thinking, the less time spent healing. Some jobs require just accepting some non-crippling scrapes and bruises, to get them over with.

Each time you are successful, the thrill of victory leads you to tackle some other impossible job on your list, causing certain injury. Beware of this feeling, and be picky about any new adventure. If you are scratched or scraped more than three times by the same job, you deserve it.

Don't tell anyone how you accomplished those impossible tasks. This is tough, but you are depriving them of memories and lessons galore, provided they survive.

Someone once said, "The difficult we do at once, the impossible takes a little longer". There are very few two man jobs that are impossible for one man to do, provided he is blessed with enough time and imagination. Phobias supply enough speed bumps to make each job interesting.

Animals and machines can make a tough job turn sour. Dogs don't have enough controls. There are no knobs to adjust their activity intensity or a steering wheel to direct it. Disaster is just around the corner. Animals have a tough time picking out the command words from the increasingly salty language as the situation deteriorates. Cows and horses are usually part of the tough job in the first place.

Machines don't know their own strength. Machines don't understand voice commands even without the cuss words. Turn a machine loose on a simple two man job and you'll be buying something, or repairing something, real soon. Unless the machine is dormant, and just part of a cobbled idea, avoid it. It'll hurt you.

If you are in the habit of throwing money at a problem, you should stop what you are doing and, get into politics where your skill can be put directly into practice, without further ado. You can tell how much pain a certain task has cost by the willingness of the entrepreneur to discuss the steps, necessary to accomplish it. If he gets mouth diarrhea, even you could do the job. If his face twitches and his eyes show distinct terror, this fellow should be revered for his execution of the impossible.

Never, ever, say. "I can do that!" It will prove to everyone listening, a weakness exists in your character. If you figure you can do the job, fine, but at least find out the path to success used. Braggarts don't last long doing two man jobs alone. Any instructions given to these fellows lack critical segments needed to evade sure pain. These experienced instructors are a brutal lot.

Education gives answers provided by someone else's experiences. Find a scarred old man, befriend him, and you will have access to a gold mine of information. If he has no scars, he's just a useless old scutter. Watch for limps, missing fingers, and dirty fingernails. These guys have been around.

If you have just finished a particular trying task and know someone who is waiting for information without pain, and he sports lily white hands, lead him astray. He'll say. "How did that exhaust job go?" "Piece of cake, man, piece of cake!" It'll be good.

"The End"

IN IT'S PROPER PLACE

I've spent a large portion of my life, either putting things in their proper place, or trying to figure out where in the devil that was. The devil is a spacious site with many little hiding places. These little crevices acquire increasingly salty names as the search progresses. Some of the names acquire salty adjectives as well. In fact, as the search continues, you have to wait longer and longer to find out what is actually being sought. If you keep a notebook handy, you can write down some of the more colorful descriptives for later use. It's downright entertaining to listen to a person with a variety of adjectives at his disposal.

I've known some special cases, and I won't mention any names, who can tell you where they put things. This must be a malady of some sort, because it is so rare. She can tell you what is in her freezer and how long it's been there. She even knows where it is in the freezer. She can sometimes give you the life history, if the object was an animal. I've been told she may even have a file on the contents. Okay, but only her first name. Marian. This kind of efficiency must be embarrassing enough without having someone advertise it. You can imagine the blow to her husband's ego, each time she's right. I'd have a drink now and then too. As for me, I have no such efficiency problem.

In far too many cases another malady is the culprit. An object may be located only when it determined where it was last used. As time goes by, the reconstruction of events becomes more difficult. I've seen people walk through past events with such determination that they forgot what they were looking for. Then I, or I mean they, must revert to the adjectives without a noun to follow. This flagrant use of improper grammar would make an English Teacher cringe.

Most lost items would not get that way if I would only have the time to build them a proper place. After that, the time saving alone, would allow me to build proper places for other people. It's tough to get together enough tools in one spot to make a proper place. A way out, perhaps, might be to buy enough tools to build a proper place for something and just let the whole thing evolve from there. Or, put video cameras everywhere to track the journey of each piece of equipment.

I've been to places where everything looks lost, but isn't. Such a place was the local Coast-To Coast store, when it was run by a fellow we'll call Greg Whitmore. The shelves were piled to the ceiling, but Greg knew where a given item was, bar none. I'd read about a brand new fishing bait, ask Greg if he would be ordering any and try to guess where he'd stuff them when they arrived. He'd never admit he was not up on all the new things, he'd just say "It's on the truck". Greg would order anything he didn't have. Sometimes it was fun just to increase his inventory.

One of my biggest headaches has been finding the proper place to file important papers. Think about it. Does car insurance papers or license go under c, i, a, l, or v. It could go under car, auto, insurance, license, or vehicle. If I did the filing, you might want to look through all the possibilities.

A tackle box has more possibilities of the proper place than there are fishermen. Most often the bait or rig you are looking for is in a central location known as the snarl. The snarl can be a great vocabulary builder depending on the amount of time available to the angler. You can tell how much time he has to spare by the volume of his verbalization.

One thing I've noticed is how attached people get to proper places. Have you ever noticed the frustration of someone who is forced to park somewhere else because his spot is taken. He will carry on worse than a cow locked out of her stall. His entire day might be ruined in one fell swoop. Airline seats, favorite chairs, fishing spots, place at table, church pews, or hunting stands can all be the basis for explosive emotional discharges. Depending on the stability of the victim, these areas should be violated with care. Pranks are fun, but bodily harm is not.

Similar chairs and parking spots, are peoples property. Lawn boundary stakes are a big thing in some peoples lives. Hammer in five or six bogus property line stakes at night, and watch a fanatic go stark raving mad during the day. Even nice guys can get in trouble by mowing a couple strips of the neighbors lawn to make yours look a little bigger. Set all your garbage cans in front of your neighbors house, or vice-versa, and watch the fun. Toss a shovel full of snow on the clean sidewalk next door for a quick lesson in psychology.

Strangers can provide entertainment for adventuresome pranksters. Reach over the shoulder of a restaurant patron, grab his pepper and salt, and walk away. He'll be upset whether he needs the pepper and salt, or not. Sit in an empty chair at someone's table. If you have some time, let a person with a full grocery cart sneak in front of you instead of going to the end of a long line. To get the best effect, now turn around and grin at the rest of the people in line.

On the open road, the drivers opinion of his proper place is equivalent to the size or cost of his vehicle, not necessarily in that order. To put cost against size, however, can be painful. If you have both, you are guaranteed your proper place.

"The End"

SNOWPLOWING ON THE NIGHT SHIFT

Plowing snow with a good loader tractor is normally pleasant, unless I'm working the night shift. Just thinking about it, makes those little hairs on my neck stand up like quills.

The new snow machine was everything we had hoped for. It plowed any snow, anywhere, wrapping the driver in the comfort of a cab. When working the night shift, however, any weaknesses are soon found or self induced.

I was plowing my mother's driveway, next door. As soon as I was all done, I thought it would be nice to widen it a little bit. "Ah, this works slick." "Whoops!" The front wheel slipped off the edge of the driveway. "No problem, I'll just back it out." The wheel just slid along the ditch, as I backed, until I managed to get into enough trouble. All this brilliant maneuvering finally dropped the hind wheel into the ditch too. Sitting at a half a bubble off plumb was starting to work me up a little. "Oh darn, son of a gun, gee whiz," is not what came to mind.

"I'll just go get the pickup and pull it out of there before it gets in there any deeper," I reasoned. The truck was too wide to drive along the side of the tractor to get behind it. I'd have to try to pull it out forward. "Shucks!" When my language gets a tad salty, Shirley goes back in the house to leave me to my own devices. When I work the night shift, what help I do get doesn't last long.

The tractor seemed like it was staked down. Yank as I might, it would not budge. My safety valve was right on the edge, but I unhooked the truck and took it out of the way. "Settle down, things could be worse", I thought. "There must be a way out of this that won't take too long," as I walked back to the tractor. The cold was nipping my ears.

Back in the tractor a super 11 to 7 idea popped into my head. These are the worst kind, because they seem so logical at the time.

"Why not drive carefully, down through the ditch, into the field, and then out of the field." Snow in the field was a foot and a half deep, more or less. Incredibly, I drove into the field with little trouble. "Now just two hundred feet to go." I'd go ahead, back up, go ahead, back up, go ahead again. Headway was being made, but much too slow when you're working 11 to 7 and need to get some sleep before going to work in a few hours.

I backed up as far as I could, shifted to a higher gear, opened the throttle, and let her go. "Varoooom!" About twenty feet past my former penetration, the wheels were windmills, and the tractor was stuck high and tight. The night shift temper was right on the edge now, the tractor stuck fifty feet off the driveway, and one hundred and fifty feet from bare ground. "Things are not looking good, but heck, they can't get much worse", I thought, trying to calm myself. I was wrong.

"Now I can get the truck, make a track back and forth till I get to the tractor, and just hook on a chain and pull it out," I reasoned. "Heck, I've been in deeper snow than this, and this is a four wheel drive."

I started backing the truck in a little at a time. Everything seemed to be going okay even though the Chevy's rear bumper was pushing the deep snow out of the way. Back and forth, back and forth, back and forth, again and again. I checked my watch. "Oh boy, look at the time!" "Well, no guts, no glory," I reasoned. I drove all the way out so I could get a good run at it.

"Varooom, vooom, vooom, vooom, voooooom," the Chevy's spring was winding tight. The north windows of Grandma's house, had the noses of her, Shirley, and my son Steve, glued to their panes.

Machine and man shot to the rear through a cloud of exploding snow. "Oh no!" When the storm settled, I forced the door open, stepped out, and sunk to the waist in the deep snow. Now, the old temper let go with abandon. I glanced toward the house in time to see Shirley's look of horror as she cupped her hands over Steve's ears.

I now had a tractor and a four wheel drive pickup stuck, a hundred feet apart, and fifty feet from any known roadway. It must have looked strange, to someone driving by, to see such a spectacle as this. Here was a cleanly plowed driveway on one side, and on the other we see a tractor and a truck out in the field. In between, we see a fellow shoveling furiously with loud verbal accompaniment, while his wife, kid and mother look out the window with ears plugged.

I could just hear the comments they might have. "What did you do that for?" You should have stayed on the driveway, heh heh." "Boy, you are really in there, bet that took some doing!" "I'd help ya, but I got a bad back." "Could you tone it down, I don't like that kind of language." "My tractor could have gotten out of there."

After about an hour both vehicles were shoveled out, put away, and I could go to bed. Sleep does not come easily after an episode like that. Soon it was time to get up and go to work again.

On the other shifts things went better. A lot of driveways were plowed without disaster.

When plowing other people's driveways, there are a few phrases to be real careful about. "The ditch isn't deep at all." "I think the edge of the driveway is right about here, somewhere." "Hey, you lopped off my bush, you got insurance?" Then there's the one that's never in time. "Look out!"

After a couple of winters, it was becoming clear, a plow for the truck would be able to do the job a lot faster. I'd still have the tractor in case it really got bad. I decided to look into getting a plow for the truck. But, that's another story.

By Dennis P. Kolb

HONDA HAVOC

The warm summer days have been further enjoyed by the breezy rides on the little Honda Express. In the seven odd years I've owned the little machine, it has been a party to several scars and scrapes. I'm sure the little red moped is not entirely to blame. In 8000 miles, one fourth of which is spent on the night shift, something is bound to happen.

Of course, there were the small jabs it inflicted on me through the years. It seemed to enjoy the malicious tricks to no end.

Lack of a gas gauge left the door open to several unprovoked attacks. It would turn its tank switch to the reserve position just to make me push it to the gas station. It says in the book that the reserve tank is good for five miles. Don't you ever believe it. When

I hit the three and a half mile mark, the little devil made me push it the last mile home.

Someone is always ready, later of course, to ask me what I was doing.

Flame got 100 miles to the gallon, but still succeeded in embarrassing me with these antics. It would even knock me in the leg a couple times while I pushed it home. I wonder why I put up with it, sometimes.

Flame was well equipped. There was a bug stopping windshield on the front, and twin baskets on the back, each big enough for a 12 pack.

I learned the hard way to keep my shirt tucked in when riding full bore at 28 miles per hour. A bee got sucked in under my shirt, and practiced his pain inflicting art, while I alternately tried to slow to a stop and beat him to death with my fist. I wondered what was making all the noise, but that stopped when I closed my mouth.

Flame gave me a bloody nose just one time. It was during the night shift week of my swing shift, you know, the tense one. I was in a hurry. I took a short cut across the summer hardened lawn at full throttle. One lousy rough spot, and Flame whacked me across the face, with the windshield, so hard I saw stars. The stars were nice, but the pain wasn't worth it. By the time I got stopped, my nose was bleeding, possibly broken, and the hurt was so intense it brought tears to my eyes. This #*#*#** moped got me again.

Shirley happened to be there, and was quick to point out how unnecessary it was to blame Flame. "Don't get blood on that new shirt."

My eyes blackened only a little, so I was in fair shape.

I kept the brakes adjusted tight, because in town, Marshfield drivers often consider cycle riders invisible. The gravel on our country road made braking no less than an adventure, but in the country panic stops are rare.

I was working the night shift again when the car radiator sprung a leak. It would be expensive to take it to a garage, and I had all the tools to do the job. This would be a good time to put on the new hoses too.

IT took quite a while to get all the screws out, the fan and shroud removed, and all the old hoses off. Before too much longer, I had the radiator out. I took the radiator to town to have it repaired.

The next day the radiator was ready and I put it back in. I didn't pull a trailer so the fan shroud could be left off. I put on the new hoses and pretty quick the job was done, and I had saved some serious coin. I was proud of myself.

I needed to look at some calves, a couple miles away, so I could take the car and check for any possible leaks at the same time.

I had not driven a mile before the steam was rolling out from under the hood. I slammed on the brakes and started to get a little heated myself. I popped the hood and got out. It did not take long to see that the fan shroud had kept the fan away from the hoses. #*#*#*#*! The fan ripped a nasty gash in my new hose. #*#*!

Wally Nennig lived near where I stopped, and was good enough to give me a ride home. I hopped in the pickup, went to Hewitt, and bought a new hose at Draxler's garage. I drove back to the car, put on the new hose, and added enough anti-freeze to fill the radiator. I could see the shroud needed to be replaced or I would be buying another hose. #*#*#*#*!

I raced back home for the fan shroud. I grabbed a couple tools, threw the fan shroud in the moped basket, and took off. I crossed the highway, hit a little bump, and the fan shroud jumped out of the basket onto the road. #*#*#*#*!

I clamped on both brakes, hard. Flame wrestled me to the gravel, hard. My leg and arm ground into the road. "This really hurts!" There is a truck coming.

I scrambled out from under the moped, and dragged it out of the way. I pushed the moped home with its busted windshield and bent handlebar. I was hurting pretty bad, but even more angry. I'd fix that car if it killed me. Both arm and leg were raw but that would have to wait.

This time I took the truck and finished fixing the car. I left the truck in Wally's yard and went to look at the calves like I had planned to do in the first place. By the time I got back home, I was starting to stiffen up from the road rash.

I took off what was left of my shirt and pants. Wow, if it's this bad at 15 miles an hour, what would it be like at 50? I'd shudder to think of it! Gravel was hanging onto the raw meat on both the arm and leg.

I started the water in the bathtub. When the tub was full, I eased my bruised body into the water. Have you ever climbed in a hot bath with a bad sunburn? This was like that, only the pain lasted somewhat longer. The long soak gave me time to reflect on a tough day.

When I went to work that night, I wore a long sleeved shirt to hide my wounds, and tried my best not to limp. Norm never suspected a thing, and it was his last day on the shift. Norm can be a brutal s.o.b. if you give him the chance. Of course, the rest of the workers on my shift took their turns trying to outdo one another with their insulting ideas.

Eventually, with daily soaks, all that was left were the scars to remind me where the pain had been. Before long, I had a new windshield, straightened the handlebars, and reset the front brake to grab a little less.

It was some weeks later when the neighbor lady, Fern Scherr brought back all the memories again. "What happened to you, out on the road out here, a couple weeks ago?" She chided. "Oh nuthin." I said.

"Bull dung", She said. "I saw you ------- fall. You almost got run over by that truck to boot!"

Flame has not attacked me in a long time. If it ever happened again, it would be too soon.

"The End"

THE NEW SNOW PLOW

Winter can be a slow time of year unless the drudgery can be broken up in a way long remembered. There is no lawn to mow or cropping to be done. You can't even paint when it's cold. It's dark a lot more, and winter can be just too boring. What could liven it up?

When it snows, there is too much to do all at one. The work is uncomfortable. The tractor has a cab now, but it takes much too long to clean out the snow. What to do?

If I had a plow on the truck, I could make a lot of money and I could write off some of the plow's cost. It would be almost like getting it free. There are some nice plows out there, plows with fancy lights, snow deflectors, and plows that go up and down and turn from side to side with a flick of a lever. Even the most expensive one would be a gold mine.

A used plow is out of the question. It must sometimes go day and night, maybe longer. Used parts might break. You get what you pay for. All the newest ideas and oldest problems will have been worked out. You don't have to paint a new one. The bank has a lot of money. A guy may as well get his share of the big money floating around with a plow that won't need repair and won't cost anything.

Shirley was bombarded with these facts until she saw the benefits too. She said, "If you want a toy that bad, buy it!" Boy, she wanted it more than I did, and still she could show that much restraint.

I ordered my new Western plow with hydra-turn, snow deflector, and the best lights available. "Wow, now I'll have it made!" I could hardly wait, and I could tell Shirley was excited too. She gets a little sarcastic when she gets excited.

The day finally came to put on the new plow. I dropped off the truck at Monroe Truck Equipment and went home to wait. The phone finally rang. "Come pick up your truck." The cost was a little more than free, but not to worry.

I was bound to find out just what this machine would do. The plow was wide,, but those other drivers sure seemed to take more than their share of the road. The control worked in all directions, and I was trying them all the way home. The Wisconsin winter has met its match.

Just before I got home, it seemed like a good idea to try to plow some snow. Down goes the plow. "Where did it go? I can't see it. Oh no, it lays right down of the road!" "Now what's wrong?" I got out and looked it all over. Looked okay to me. Tried it again. Same thing. "Now I'm mad, and they're going to find out just who they're dealing with."

I stormed into the house and called up Monroe Truck. "The plow doesn't work. It lays down on the road." "Did you tighten the springs?" "What springs?" "The springs on the back of the plow," he says. "Oh ya, heh heh, I kind of figured that was it." He would have showed more class if he had hung up the phone before he started laughing. "That hinder!"

Every day I got better with the plow, and my confidence soon outdistanced my ability. When you drive into a snow bank too far with a plow, you have made a memorable mistake, especially if you are alone. (Since Shirley claimed she could read my lips while I was out there plowing, my son, Steve was not allowed to ride along to, "hear that kind of language".)

After entering the snow bank, a stout shovel, if you have one, and a half hour later, you are back on the road. One stout shovel is now standard equipment, unless it's forgotten. If the shovel is forgotten, a great test of patience will bare its ugly fangs.

When a wheel slips off the edge of a driveway, you are quickly in deep fertilizer. This can be true even if you remembered the shovel. Four wheel drive doesn't help if the wheels can't touch the ground. This trick is good for a dandy delay and a heated expression of strong feelings. The fellow who pulls you out always takes advantage of the situation. "You trying to plow the ditch? Heh heh." "Should I follow you around for a while? Heh heh." "How wide did you think the driveway was? Heh heh" "What a hinder!"

One morning, to get an early start, I began plowing at 3:30 A.M.. Nobody can get in the way cause nobody is up that early. The plowing was going pretty well, about two miles form home and about ten below zero. Pretty soon the headlights looked a little crooked. "Fwump, fwump, fwump. Oh no! I've got a flat tire! A #*#*#*#* flat tire!" I never carried a spare on the truck. It was home, but where? "I wish it wasn't so far away. I wish it wasn't four A.M.. I wish somebody was around, and I wish it wasn't so #*#*#*- cold!"

By the time I walked home, I was firmly convinced the spare tire could not be found, and if it could, surely the tractor wouldn't start, and I'd just go back to bed and forget the whole thing.

What rotten luck! The tire was right out in the open. The old Oliver77 had the nerve to start immediately. I chucked the tire into the loader bucket and headed back to the Equine Center. I changed the tire and left the tractor parked in the parking lot. Of course there wasn't time to get the tractor home in time to avoid the abuse to follow. "What did you need the tractor for? Heh heh." "Spare tires are handy when you got em, heh heh heh." "Hinder!"

When plowing after dark and angling the plow a lot, much strain is put on the old battery. One time is too much to have the engine kill, and not have enough left in the battery to start again. "Arrghh!"

Now we're getting real good with the plow. Let's impress someone. "I'll just angle the plow and clean some of the snow away from the building. "Woorrmph!" "Wow, you took the mirror right off!" "She really slammed against the building in a hurry! You took a good chunk out of the building too! Nice work, haw haw haw." "Hinder!"

It always seems to snow when I'm on the 11 to 7 shift when I'm running about a click short. I do what I can in the morning, but after being up all night, it's not much. Of course, no one sleeps during the day. "If you need to get plowed, give Denny a call and just let it ring, heh heh heh." "Stupid inconsiderate #*#*#* hinder!"

"The End"

CHRISTMAS DAY LADDER ATTACK

When the night was finally wrestled to its knees, Christmas morning arrived. Another 11 to 7 at the power plant was history. I managed to stay awake and reasonably alert during Father Bornbach's thirty five minute Mass at 8 o'clock. Father says: "If I see anyone sleeping, I've talked long enough."

When I got up on Christmas Day there was no clue of the suffering I would endure on this festive day.

It was just after noon, cold, and after a three hour nap, things drag a little. I sat with my coffee, looking at the tree, gathering my wits, and easing into the day. Everything is in super slow motion and super aggravating to watch, or so I'm told. Cleaned up, shaved, and dressed, we're rolling now.

It looked like snow, so the truck should be put in the shed. The big door balked. One bracket, atop the twelve foot door, was cocked a little, making it tough to slide open. Slipping on the ice, and almost down, brought forth a passionate ardor of profanity that even surprised me. I backed the truck into its spot.

When closing the door was even more difficult, it only seemed right, to get the ladder and fix it right away. I put up the ladder while trying to decide what tool would work best. That tool wasn't there. I finally grabbed a big pliers and huffed outside.

It's a good thing I spent a large chunk of life, following Bratt Mitten around, while he handled similar frustrating tasks. It expanded my vocabulary enough to be never at a loss for words, except in the company of women, children, and certain others. Bratt had served under George Patton and polished his art over time.

I climbed the ladder knowing I had the wrong tool. On 11 to 7 you are not slowed by such trivia. I started wiggling the roller bracket and then I was on the ground.

Things happened so fast that the sequence of events gets a little blurred. It seems ladder bottoms will slide uphill a little when they're on glare ice. On 11 to 7 there is no time for precautions, push on. One nearby might have heard the familiar, "Arrrgh!", on the way down. But, had I jumped off the roof, it would not have taken more time to hit the ground.

I was looking at the ground and speechless!

There is pain!

Knees pain, elbows pain, face pain, left thumb pain, right hand pain, and maybe another finger hurts.

I rolled off the ladder still beneath me, and found every body part still worked. Nobody home but me. The ladder had to be dragged inside in case of snow. With that job done, I hucked toward the house, feeling shock and nausea creeping up on me.

In the house, I tried to assess the damage. The knee was real big already. Must get ice on it. Need rest first with feet higher than head to calm down a little. This kind of hurt changes your mind from swear to prayer in a hurry.

After settling down enough to get up and get the ice out and bagged, it was back to horizontal to lick my wounds.

In a little while, Shirley and Steve came home. "What happened to you?" she said. "What were you trying to do?" "Can't I trust to leave you alone?" These were all questions Shirley wanted an answer to.

While I took about an hour to recover a little, they assessed the damage and shut the shed door. It seems my big knee had mashed the ladder rung quite flat. The nasty scratch on my face pointed toward a blackening eye.

We managed to get to Shirley's parent's house in time for pot luck supper. I could walk but was afraid to sit down right away. Everyone marveled at how lucky I was. I was so lucky that it was almost miraculous. Why, any luckier and I'd be dead, or at the very least, a bleeding broken wreck hanging in traction somewhere.

After the party, it was home to bed for a couple of hours, and back to work. By now, more muscles ached and big patches of black and blue were blooming. It was great! I was finally beginning to look as bad as I felt.

Of course, anything remotely aggravating is picked up on right away by fellow 11 to 7 ers. I was considered lucky, lucky, lucky until it was long past old.

Well over a month later, 11 to 7 is gone again, but healing is not complete. Even though these mistakes are not repeated, there are always new ones, it seems. The blackened thumbnail is a long reminder as it grows out. In the wrong company, it gives real fuel for abuse. Maybe that's why a certain rock star wears one glove. He doesn't have to hear: "What did you do there?" "Wow, how big was the hammer?" "Bet that hurt. Feel stupid, don't ya?"

Maybe some nice flesh colored nail polish would work. Maybe I could paint them all black. Things sure look different on 11 to 7.

By Dennis P. Kolb

STICK WELDER

Over the past couple of years, it has become increasingly apparent that I could save, and even make, some money, with a good welder. When something needs welding, no matter how simple, it's going to cost time and money. I can weld.

Sure, it had been about thirty years since I struck an arc in Mr. Ader's metalwork class. As I remember, welding came easy. It was like gluing with metal. I already know how to do it. It's like riding a bike. I used quite a few metalworking tools in that class, with good grades too. A simple welder would be a piece of cake.

Boy, I had seen some real bird-crap welding through the years. I remember how nice my welding looked back then. The only way to get some things done well, is to do them yourself. Custom welding is always in demand. It seems that if you do something well, there is always a need for it.

I looked over all the welders on the market. The new wire-feed welders were impressive and easy to use. They were expensive. The old A.C. Buzz Boxes were cheap, but not versatile enough. The A.C.*D.C. models seemed a perfect choice since I was already proficient in their use. If I could do it thirty years ago, I can do it now. Maybe not as often, but I can do it.

I bought a new A.C.*D.C. welder. In a couple hours I was ready to weld.

The new machine seemed a tad defective. My first piece of metal looked like a porcupine. There were 7 or 8 welding rods sticking to it at awkward angles. Part of the problem was seeing through the cheap welding helmet. I couldn't see anything before it was too late. Maybe the welding rods were no good. I got the bolt cutter and cut the quills off the metal plate. I kept my mouth shut to avoid an earache.

My brother borrowed the welder. I had a guinea pig. I would find out if the welder worked. Funny, it worked for him. He sensed my surprise, and mentioned he had taken a refresher welding course.

When the welder was back in my shop, I had another go at it. I cranked up the amps. A book, I looked at, suggested raising the amperage if the rod stuck to the work. Some of the small points slipped my mind since high school.

My first project was a garbage burner made from a 275 gallon heating oil barrel. I bolted as much as I could. The rest needed to be welded. I needed to weld some pipe flanges to the pipe legs to serve as feet for the burner.

I touched the ark to the pipe. The amps were a little high. I blew a hole in the pipe big enough to drop a golf ball through. Another length of pipe that size was conveniently handy. After a few adjustments, the welder was putting out some decent bird-crap.

I burned up about ten sticks, welding feet on the pipes. When I was done, I sat back and admired the fine job. It wasn't too pretty, but there were no holes and not one stuck welding rod. All that was left to do was slag removal. It looked much the same, when I was done chipping away the slag, as it had before I started.

I lifted one end of the burner to reposition it for further construction. I was amazed. I had just gone through ten welding rods. When I lifted the burner, its legs pulled out of their shoes. How could I have welded that long without getting anything to stick together? This is one of the times I would have paid to be an observer instead of the participant. It would have been hilarious. As it was, it wouldn't be funny for about a week.

I took all the legs off the burner and hired the welding done. When anyone asks me who did the welding, I don't tell an outright lie. I just point at my welder and let them draw their own conclusions.

I have welded a few things that held for a while, but nothing I'd stake my life on. Some clowns I know seem to get a read wallop out of my metal construction. It is usually bolted and welded. Heck, I've seen fellows wear a belt and suspenders. Some people are more thorough than others.

Maybe there is a spot open, somewhere, for a welding critic. I have seen more bad welds than I could count. Some of them were made by others. The terminology used to describe the welds is also fresh in my mind, some of it quite demeaning. Most of the remarks include animal bodily waste as a literary tool.

One show-off welder I know claims he can weld anything from the crack of dawn to a broken heart. Hog-wash, I say. Prove it! They can't!

To tell me that my welding clamps hold longer than my welds, was in bad taste. This sort of remark is uncalled for. I know I didn't call for it.

Welding practice continues in the privacy of my small shop. I'm buying less bolts and more welding rods. I've got a helmet that lets me see the welding better. Better welding rods and a couple other accessories are now in stock. In other words, I threw some money at the problem.

"The End"